BEAS'

Remo and Chiun [...]
coming from the [...]
the heavy steel-plate door, they saw only a
man and a woman standing quietly inside.
Their faces wore small smiles. Their hands
were folded ceremoniously before them.

Then they moved away from each other.

Between them, on the floor, was a puddle of
blood, in which floated a broken human skull.

"The wallpaper is red," Remo said, noticing
it for the first time.

"It is not paper. It is blood," Chiun said.

The man and the woman came toward Remo.
Vapors of foul-smelling gas belched from their
mouths along with deep growls so loud and low
that they seemed to shake the walls.

The Destroyer had heard about men and
women getting animal together—but this was
too much. . . .

THE DESTROYER #61

LORDS OF THE EARTH

The Destroyer #61

LORDS OF THE EARTH

WARREN MURPHY & RICHARD SAPIR

A SIGNET BOOK

NEW AMERICAN LIBRARY

PUBLISHER'S NOTE

These novels are works of fiction. Names, characters, places, and incidents either are the product of the author's imagination or are used fictitiously, and any resemblance to actual persons, living or dead, events, or locales is entirely coincidental.

NAL BOOKS ARE AVAILABLE AT QUANTITY DISCOUNTS WHEN USED TO PROMOTE PRODUCTS OR SERVICES. FOR INFORMATION PLEASE WRITE TO PREMIUM MARKETING DIVISION, NEW AMERICAN LIBRARY, 1633 BROADWAY, NEW YORK, NEW YORK 10019.

SIGNET, SIGNET CLASSIC, MENTOR, PLUME, MERIDIAN and NAL BOOKS are published by New American Library, 1633 Broadway, New York, New York 10019

First printing, May, 1985

1 2 3 4 5 6 7 8 9

PRINTED IN THE UNITED STATES OF AMERICA

Prologue

"In the end, it will be the insects who rule the earth."
—Noted scientist.

"In the end, who cares?"—Remo Williams, identity and address unknown, fingerprints on file nowhere, former policeman, still recorded in some old newspaper files as the last man to be executed in the electric chair in the New Jersey State Penitentiary.

"End? What end? You whites will be with us forever."
—Chiun, Master of Sinanju, vessel of the sun source of all the Martial Arts, His Awesome Magnificence, known as "Little Father" by Remo Williams, who is a white, but one of the nice ones at times. Not all the time, however. And lately, even less frequently, if you could believe that. Not that complaining ever did any good.

1

Winston Hoag was afraid of many things in life, but never the thing that killed him.

He was afraid of the sudden air eddies that came up over tree lines on warm days and sent his small single-engine plane into a sudden dive until, only feet above the cotton fields, he was able to wrestle back control of the craft.

He was afraid of the chemicals he released over the fields, afraid that constant contact with the pesticides that protected the crops for the farmer would somehow get into his blood system and kill him.

He was afraid of losing his contracts as a crop duster and afraid of seeing his family go on welfare. He thought he would rather kill himself than let that happen, although he did not know if he had the courage to kill himself.

He was afraid also that his plane would come apart one day because Winston Hoag always had to measure the cost of new parts against the cost of sending his children to a good school, of his wife being able to put good food on the table, of being able to help support his aging parents.

He was afraid of sunsets that played games with his

6

depth perception and afraid of sunrises that could suddenly blind a pilot in an open-air cockpit.

But one thing he was not afraid of was the young couple who offered him two hundred dollars to let them install a video camera between his legs to shoot upward and film his face as he dusted crops.

All he wanted was to make sure that the camera didn't get in the way of his foot controls.

"We want you to turn on the camera before you get your chemical valves to release," said the young woman. "This is important. We want your spraying system off until you have the camera on for at least a minute."

"Two minutes," corrected the young man who was with her.

"Sure," said Winston Hoag. "But why?"

"Because that's how we want it," said the woman. She was an ash blond and spoke with the long vowels of wealth, with the casual, confident air that made her look rich in a pair of faded blue jeans. If Winston Hoag wore faded jeans, he knew he would just look poor. In fact, the first thing he'd done when he enlisted in the Air Force had been to throw away his old faded jeans. And when he was discharged, one of the first things he did was buy brand-new jeans, stiff blue-black ones, spanking new, and uncomfortable.

Winston Hoag, like many people who had been dirt poor when they were young, always dreaded returning to that. He could use the two hundred dollars.

"If that's how you want it, that's how you'll get it," he said, "but I would like to know why."

"Because," said the woman.

"Because we want to get the change in your

expression from when you're not spraying to when you are," the young man explained.

"There ain't no change," said Hoag.

"There is," said the woman. "There has to be."

"Actually, we don't know," the man said. He wore sandals and khaki-colored shorts with a lot of buckles on them, and carried a roll of hundred-dollar bills. "We'd like to find out." His old T-shirt called for saving the timber wolf from extinction. Its legend read: "Extinct is forever."

Winston Hoag could go along with that. He didn't like to see animals die out. And the animal he would least like to see die out was himself.

He took the two hundred dollars.

"Remember," the woman said, "A full two minutes before you turn on your chemical spray, we want the camera between your legs turned on."

"Okay," Hoag said.

"How do you protect your insecticide tanks?" the young man asked.

"What?"

"What protection do you use for your insecticide tanks?"

"Don't use nothing," Hoag said. "I'm the one who needs protection."

"How do you know your insecticide tanks won't release prematurely?"

"They're safe from that."

"Let me see," said the woman.

"They're just plain old insecticide tanks," said Hoag.

"We want to see them anyway," the young man said.

Hoag took them to the plane, and explained that he had more than adequate safety measures to protect the tanks from premature release.

"You've got to remember," he said. "That insecticide costs money and I could be sued if I sprayed some residential area."

"Yes," the woman said. "We know that money means a lot to you."

"Listen, I can use the money," Hoag said. "But everybody's got to earn a living and I don't rightly take no job with insults attached."

"We understand," the young man said soothingly. "We didn't mean to insult you. Could you possibly reinforce the insecticide tanks?"

"Sir?" said Hoag, trying to be polite in turn.

"Could you reinforce the insecticide tanks, sort of put another set of brackets around them?"

"Not for no two hundred dollars," Hoag said.

"Three hundred," said the young man.

Hoag shook his head. First of all, the new metal might cost another hundred and that would add weight to the plane and cut his fuel economy. He was ready to forget the whole thing right there. There were a lot of things he would do for a few hundred dollars, but taking risks with an old plane was not among them.

By the time the crop duster and the young couple worked out exactly how they wanted the insecticide tanks protected, it added two hundred pounds of weight to the plane, threw off its balance and would cost the couple no less than fifteen hundred dollars. Winston Hoag was sure they would refuse.

But the hundreds just kept coming from a roll of bills in the young man's hand. And they didn't even want a receipt.

"You know," said Hoag, "even if this danged plane crashes, those tanks won't be harmed. Darn, if they aren't the most secure things this side of Fort Knox."

"You're sure?" the woman said.

"I wish I was that well protected," said Hoag, and the couple flashed simultaneous smiles.

They came back the next day to inspect his work. They insisted on installing the camera, setting it just so, and demanded to see where he sat in the plane. They readjusted the camera's angle to make sure, they said, that the lens got his face perfectly.

"I think it's pointing at my chest," said Hoag as the young woman ran her hand down between his legs. He liked the touch of her hands so he didn't complain.

"We know what we're doing," she said. "Now, let's see you reach forward for the switch."

He leaned down and reached for the shiny metal toggle switch which looked as if it had been removed from an old electric motor. It had been soldered onto the trigger of the video camera.

As he touched the switch, his chest was less than two feet away from the camera lens.

"Perfect," said the woman.

Hoag took off that afternoon to dust a small crop of peanuts outside Plains, Georgia, fifteen hundred dollars richer from two young people he thought of as fools.

He wasn't even going to bother dusting that day. He didn't want to risk going tight to the peanut field, skimming close to trees with the plane's extra weight. He planned to get over the peanut field, turn on the camera, fly absolutely level for twenty minutes so the camera wouldn't catch anything but his face and the sky, and the two rich idiots would never know he hadn't been dusting. Then he would fly back, give them their camera, remove the heavy junk from the plane and do the regular peanut-dusting run the next day.

"A fool and his money are soon parted," thought Hoag as he reached two thousand feet and leveled his single-engine plane. Then he leaned down into the cockpit, smiled at the camera lens, and tightly grabbed the toggle switch. He was still smiling as the camera lens shot forward like a projectile, driving directly into his heart with enough force to shatter his sternum and explode it throughout his chest cavity.

The coroner never figured this out, though, because there wasn't very much left of Winston Hoag when the pieces of everything were picked up off the red-clay dust of the Georgia field.

The plane's wings were shredded, the fuselage was junk, and Winston Hoag resembled bones held together by blood clots. The only things that emerged unscathed from the wreck were the reinforced insecticide tanks, two bright metal cylinders that looked like unexploded bombs.

Eyewitnesses said that Hoag had been flying at about two thousand feet, very level and steady, when the plane suddenly went into a crazy spin and flew into the ground at top speed, narrowly missing a peanut farmer who had his eyes on a rabbit that he thought ready to attack him.

It was only when the local television station got an anonymous phone tip that the coroner found out it had been a murder and not just an accident.

"If you look for a camera lens," said the caller, "you'll find that it has been shot into the chest of mass murderer Winston Hoag."

"Mass murderer? Who did Hoag murder?" asked the reporter, desperately signaling someone to get the police to trace the call.

"Everything," said the telephone voice. "He murdered the mornings, the chirps of birds and the loping beauty of the endangered timber wolf. He murdered our water and our sky. Most of all, he murdered tomorrow."

"He was just a crop duster," the television man said.

"Exactly," said the caller. "We are the SLA and you're not going to do this to us anymore. Neither you nor the other Winston Hoags of this world."

Why would the Symbronese whatever-it-was want to murder a crop duster? thought the TV reporter.

His question was answered without even being asked.

"We are the Animal Liberation Alliance," said the caller. "It was a moral killing."

"It's moral to kill the father of three kids?" said the reporter losing his dispassionate professionalism and was yelling into the telephone.

"Yes. We crashed a plane and took a pilot without adding further trauma to the environment. The insecticide tanks did not release their genocidal poison."

In the next month, there were three other "moral killings." The Species Liberation Alliance took credit for strangling a cattle rancher with his own barbed wire. They did not, as they carefully pointed out in phone calls to the press, leave the barbed wire around for animals to cut themselves on, but instead imbedded it all in the rancher's throat. The SLA also wrapped the crew of a tuna boat in their own nets and sank them in the Pacific, off Baja, California, in such a way that the net would never break loose to trap any more fish. And they capped an oil well in Georges Bank off the Massachusetts coast with the crushed skulls of the drilling crew, proudly proclaiming that they had used a "natural nonpolluting plug."

Waldron Perriweather III did not attempt to justify the killings. After each one, he appeared on several television programs to explain his position on the deaths:

"While I disapprove of violence in any form, we have to look at the root causes of these murders." And then he lectured for a half-hour on the cruelty of man to other living creatures.

"What sort of society are we," he asked, "that would say of cruelty, 'he treated someone like a bug'? Or a worm. We impale living creatures on barbed metal hooks to bait other living creatures that we ensnare and then suffocate to death, and call it sport. I am talking, gentlemen, about fishing."

"We understand that, Mr. Perriweather," said the commentator. "Particularly in your position as America's leading protector of nature. But what about murdering an entire rigging crew?"

"What about the millions of deaths every day that a biased press does not report? After all, what is the Species Liberation Alliance trying to do but bring to the public's attention the atrocities done in their name with government support."

"What atrocities?" asked the interviewer, and on national television, Waldron Perriweather III, heir to the Perriweather fortune, a handsome blond man whose delicate features were the result of Perriweather money always marrying beauty, listed the atrocities done with American money. Mass murder of insects. Poisoning of fish and air. Legalized murder of moose called hunting.

Waldron Perriweather III had little use for those groups that merely protected the obviously lovable, like pets, birds and beautiful animals.

"What about the Inga worm?" he asked. "Around the clock, scientists are working to find a spray that will stop this creature's respirations. It reminds me of the Nazi gas ovens."

"Doesn't the Inga worm destroy crops?" he was asked.

"So does man," said Perriweather.

"How does man destroy crops?"

"The same way the Inga worm does. He eats them," Perriweather said. "But when the Inga worm attempts to share the bounty of the earth, we feverishly try to destroy it with chemicals. It is about time we stopped our human-centered biases. We must all share this earth together or we will lose it together."

On that note, he left the studio to polite applause.

But some of the newsmen were talking about the need for a new awareness of lesser creatures, and some in the audience nodded their heads approvingly. For one who did not condone the killing of Winston Hoag or the cattle rancher or the drilling crew whose families had to bury the headless bodies in closed coffins, Waldron Perriweather III had done much to promote the SLA's cause.

Perriweather returned to his palatial estate in Beverly, Massachusetts, a giant rock fortress set on a hill overlooking the Atlantic, in an area the Perriweathers had ruled for more than a century and a half. There were no lawns around the Perriweather mansion only high grass where birds and insects could nest. No pesticides ever touched the Perriweather fields.

Any servant caught using a repellent during mosquito season would be fired. Nor did the Perriweathers use netting to deter mosquitoes, preferring instead what they called the "humane approach." This involved having servants staying up all night fanning the Perriweathers so that the gentle breezes would not let a mosquito land on Perriweather flesh. Of course the servants, in truest Perriweather tradition, worked during the day as well. Just because the Perriweather family showed morality toward insects did not mean that they were financially foolish. There were, after all, limits to one's sense of decency.

At the entrance of the estate, Perriweather's Rolls-Royce halted. The chauffeur bent over and Waldron climbed onto his back to be carried by foot to the great stone mansion. Waldron did not like driving on the estate because he did not believe in spewing oil exhaust into the air of his "fellow residents," namely the flies, worms and mosquitoes.

This day, he was especially anxious to reach the main building, so he kicked his heels into the chauffeur's flanks to get him to run faster. He didn't understand what was wrong with the chauffeur when the elderly man broke out into a terrible sweat, and at the steps, he bucked and convulsed, almost knocking Perriweather to the ground.

Waldron stepped over the stricken man, commenting to the butler that he wondered where the driver had been trained. Then Waldron rushed into a rear room of the mansion, sealed by an iron door, and with netting that closed on both the inside and outside.

Air ducts fed the room. They were also sealed by fine mesh netting. The temperature was a perfect 85 degrees. Ripe fruit and spoiling meat made the air so heavy with decay that Waldron felt he could swim in it.

A white-haired man in a white coat was leaning over a microscope, looking at a petri dish. He perspired profusely in the heat and every once in a while he would spit into a bucket. He had complained once that the air was so foul he could taste it and, once tasting it, he couldn't keep his meals down.

"I'm paying enough so you can be fed intravenously," Waldron Perriweather III had reminded him, and the scientist stopped complaining.

"Is it ready yet?" Perriweather asked.

"Not yet," said the scientist. "These are just the eggs."

"Let me see," Perriweather said anxiously.

The scientist stepped aside and Perriweather leaned down until the miscroscope eyepiece touched his lashes. Then he saw them—wiggling, white and large, the most adorable things he had ever seen.

"They're lovely," Perriweather said. "They will be all right, won't they?"

"Them?"

"Of course them. They will be all right, won't they?" Perriweather snapped.

"Mr. Perriweather, I don't think you really have to worry about those maggots."

Perriweather nodded and looked back into the eyepiece, focusing on the dish of maggots eating away at rotten meat.

"Kootchy, kootchy, coo," said Waldron Perriweather III.

2

His name was Remo and he knew old buildings the way a doctor knew blood vessels. He could not remember when he had started to know them this way, to understand how builders' minds worked and where they would put passages or where they had to have spaces or felt that they needed spaces.

It was only after he had known it a long time that he realized he could see a building and know how to penetrate its hidden places, just as surely as a physician would know there was a vein under a forearm.

He knew there would be an old dumbwaiter channel in this basement and he knew that it would be behind the elevator. He also knew that a seemingly solid wall would hide it. He pressed the heel of his right hand against the plaster, feeling its dryness, sensing the darkness around him, tasting that never-lost smell of coal in this basement in Boston's Back Bay.

He pressed with his hand, steadily increasing the force so there would be no violent noise, and then the basement wall gave way with a little groan. The old dumbwaiter was inside. Carefully he gathered up the plaster in his hands, like a silent eagle with soft talons,

and gently funneled the plaster chips and dust into a
pile at his feet.

He reached inside the hole and felt old iron, ridged
with rust, that crumbled in his hands. That was the
handle for the dumbwaiter door. He did not bother to
pull it. He sensed that it would come off in his hands,
so he pressed it silently into the old wood, and it gave
way with a gentle sputter of dry rot.

These dumbwaiters had once been used by delivery
boys who were not allowed into the main halls of the
old Back Bay brownstones. They were boxes running
on pulleys. A boy would put a package of groceries
into the box, pull down on a rope, and the box would
be raised to the correct floor.

As in most of the sealed dumbwaiters, the box and
rope had long ago settled to the floor. Now there was
just a dark, airless passage, and Remo moved into it
smoothly, knowing that the brick he felt under his
hands could crumble from too much pressure. He did
not climb the brick, but instead let the wall become
part of him, creating the movement upward.

He was a thin man with thick wrists and wore a
dark T-shirt and dark slacks. His shoes were simple
loafers that skimmed gently upward as his body rose in
the narrow dark channel. And then he heard the voices
on the other side of the wall.

He made a bridge of five fingers with his left hand,
set the right hand against the opposite wall and stayed
suspended to listen. The rising was not the hard part in
dealing with heights. All movements had their own
power, but a stagnant body would fall, so he supported himself with his hands, varying the pressure
under his fingertips to maintain the unity of his motion
with the brick.

He heard one man say, "What can go wrong?
What? Tell me."

"I'm scared, I'm telling you. I'm scared. Look at the size of it. I just want to run. Forget what we found and thank our lucky stars they don't know it yet."

The first man laughed.

"Baby," he said. "We have never been so safe in our lives. It's not a crime. *They're* committing the crime. They're the ones who are outside of the law, not us. They're the ones who should be afraid. They should be pissing their pants."

"I don't know. I still say forget it."

"Look, nothing can happen to us."

"These aren't our files," the second man said.

"So?"

"We got them by accident on a computer scan by one of our research people."

"You've just proven," the first man said, "that we did not steal anything."

"But it's not ours."

"Possession is ninety percent of the law. If these files, these beautiful files, aren't ours, whose are they?"

"They belong to that sanitarium we traced in Rye, New York. Folcroft Sanitarium."

"I talked to the director up there today. He said the files aren't his."

"Well, how about that computer setup in St. Martin? That was tied up with this whole thing, somehow."

"St. Martin. Swell, a vacation island in the Caribbean. Think anybody there will care about these files?"

"I think the files at Folcroft are duplicated on St. Martin. Probably to stop them from being erased by mistake. And I think it's some secret government outfit and we ought to stay the hell away from it," the second man said.

"We'll help them stay secret. We won't say anything. We'll just become rich as Croesus from all this wonderful information."

The second man let out a sound like a soft groan. "You know, all that data tracks crime in America. The printouts have files on how somebody gave the FBI, the narcotics people and local cops the information to help send crooks to jail. I think it's our own government's attempt to keep the country from falling apart, and darn it, I think we ought to leave them alone. This country's been good to us. If some secret agency helps it survive, then let it be."

"Why?" the first man said.

"Because tampering is wrong. These people are trying to do good. What are we going to do? Make some more money? This country has already let us become rich."

"Not a good enough reason. You got to show me how I can be hurt."

"What if they have commandos or something working for them?" the second man said.

"No. The computer said only one man was authorized to do any violence."

"Maybe that one guy's dangerous."

The first man laughed aloud. "We've got three men outside the door and three men on the street. The doors are made of reinforced steel. Let's see him try something. There'll only be one dead body. His."

"I still don't like it," the second man said.

"Look, we'll be richer than oil sheiks. We can forget our computer business. We'll know all the dirt that goes on in the country. We can blackmail the government. Or people who are breaking the law. We can do anything we want and everybody'll be afraid of us and pay us. Nothing can happen to us."

Right, Remo thought to himself. These were the right ones.

He released his left hand and let his left side brace against the wall, and with an easy extension moved the room wall right into the room. Rolling free of the white plaster dust, he found himself in a high-ceilinged room with an ornate black marble fireplace and two frightened men.

Between them was a gray metal box which Remo had been told was a two-hundred-megabyte hard disk, whatever that was.

The two men were middle-aged with deep tans from some sunny place they had apparently visited that winter. But when the wall opened up and Remo came through, the tans disappeared. and they became old men with very white faces.

"This the two-hundred-megabyte hard disk?" Remo asked.

They both nodded. Their eyes were wide and their heads moved as stiffly as if their necks were petrified wood.

"That's it, huh?" confirmed Remo. He remembered Smith's computers at Folcroft, taking up most of a basement, and he didn't understand how anything of value could be contained in the small gray box.

The men nodded again.

"You make any backups?" Remo asked. He had been told to ask that and find the backups if they had made any.

"No," said both men in unison.

Remo grabbed one by the left pinky and pressed the finger backward with increasing pain.

"In the bathroom," the man gasped.

"What's in the bathroom?"

"Soft disks. Backups."

"Show me," said Remo. Both men went to a white door around the corner from the fireplace. When they opened it, Remo saw thousands of thin, recordlike disks.

"Is that it?" Remo said.

"You couldn't be from that place if you don't recognize a floppy disk," said the more aggressive of the two men. He wore a flared gray suit and a striped tie. The other wore a dark blue suit and plain white shirt with all the joy of someone rehearsing for his own funeral.

"I'm from that place," Remo said.

In his pocket was something he was supposed to use now. It was a small device that looked like a cigarette lighter but had no flame. It was black and metallic and had a button he was supposed to press. He pressed and the light in the living room flickered strangely.

"He's from that place," said the man in the flared suit. "He erased everything with a projected magnetic field."

"Is that what I did?" Remo asked.

"What are you going to use on the hard disk? It's got a platinum shell five times harder than steel."

"Five times, you say?" The men stared, stunned, at what they saw. It appeared as if the thin man in the dark shirt and trousers just slapped the two sides of the super-strong metal box, not hard, not even fast, as if he were giving it a love tap. With a crack, the shell shattered and the insides were exposed, shining purple.

Remo had been told that the insides, the hard disk, was vulnerable even to a nudge because of its incredible closeness to some sort of internal reading device. A tap would disable it. He gave it a punch, and a shower of glittery material sprayed the room.

The two men now realized that their own door's

protective thickness prevented their bodyguards from hearing them.

"That it?" asked the bolder man. He had a small pistol he had been carrying since that first day when his computers had somehow been switched into the mind of the master computer that had monitored the dark side of America for so long.

"No," Remo said. "Two more things."

"What?" said the man. He had his hand on the pistol. He would put a shot right into the thin man's dark shirt. He would not aim for the head. Nothing fancy. A simple bullet in the chest, then unload the gun into the head and run. That was his plan. Unfortunately, it required an operating brain to carry it out and his was suddenly in the back part of the fireplace.

The other man passed out and never recovered, since his spinal column had been neatly severed. Neither of them had seen Remo's hand move for the very simple reason that they weren't supposed to.

Remo looked around. "Hard disk, backup," he mumbled to himself. "Hard disk, backup. That's it. I think I got it."

He left by the dumbwaiter. Outside, in the alley next to the elegant Back Bay brownstone, an armed guard gave him a hard stare. Remo smiled. The guard asked him what he was doing coming out of the building.

Remo tried to think of an answer. He didn't really have a good one so he deposited the guard and his gun in a nearby garbage container called a Dempsey Dumpster.

Had he missed anything? Hard disk, backup. That's what he was supposed to destroy. He was sure of it. Maybe.

He did not like the world of computers.

He liked it even less when he arrived at a small resort off the South Carolina coast. Several wood bungalows faced the calm Altantic, lapping against sand and grass. The old wooden steps of the bungalow made no sound as he moved lightly up them. The air was salty and good. Remo whistled softly, but once inside, he stopped. An ugly glass screen atop a keyboard was staring at him. Someone had brought a computer into the bungalow.

Sitting in a chair facing the sea was a frail wisp of a man in a subdued maroon kimono with gold dragons dancing around a golden sunburst. At the sides of his head, gentle fluffs of hair floated like wool grass in a breeze. Two parchment-frail hands with delicate fingers and long graceful fingernails rested peacefully at his side.

"Who brought that thing in here?" asked Remo, pointing to the computer near the front door.

"It makes my heart sing at the joy of your return," said the old man, Chiun, Master of Sinanju.

"I'm sorry, Little Father," said Remo. "I just hate computers and machines and things that don't go bump in the night."

"That is no excuse to greet me with such irreverence," Chiun snapped.

"Sorry," said Remo.

He walked around behind the computer and saw a body lying on the floor. There was an open attaché case next to it.

"What's this all about?" Remo asked. He saw a brochure for a computer inside the attaché case.

"What?" Chiun asked mildly.

"This body. Did you have some trouble with the computer?" Remo asked.

"I did not. I am not a computer illiterate."

"Then what's this corpse doing here?"

"*He* had trouble with the computer," Chiun explained.

"It up and killed him?"

"He's dead, isn't he?" said Chiun.

"I am not getting rid of this body," Remo said.

Chiun was silent. Had he asked Remo to get rid of the body? Had he done anything this day, this poor sunlit day where the world had little joy for him, but attempt to be reasonable and fair with this highly unfair world? What had he ever asked from the world? He wanted peace. He wanted only a small dollop of fairness and a chance to enjoy whatever the sun might bring. In return for giving Remo the awesome secrets of Sinanju, Chiun, the Master of Sinanju, received no gratitude but hostile questions about some worthless computer salesman who had died because he had failed with the computer.

Through the years, he thought with bitterness, he had given Remo what no other white man had been given. He had given him the power of Sinanju, the sun source of all the martial arts, from which had come the lesser rays that even whites had mastered: karate, tae kwando, judo, and all the other weak movings of the body.

And for giving this to Remo, for training him to masterhood, Chiun had received nothing, as always. But he was determined this morning not to allow this to ruin the day. He would accept as a fact that some things, some defects of character, could not be overcome, no matter how perfect and wondrous the training or the trainer. Chiun was determined to let Remo's rudeness pass until he realized that Remo was going to let it pass also, and then he had no choice but to bring up the ingratitude, the rudeness, the insensitivity, and all the other things he hadn't wanted to mention.

"I'm not cleaning up this body," Remo said. "I don't ask you to take care of my bodies, so please don't ask me to take care of yours."

"This one is not mine," said Chiun. "But I realize there are some things that can never be explained to one with a vicious heart."

"Since when do I have a vicious heart, Little Father?" Remo asked.

"You have always had a vicious heart."

"I'm used to 'ungrateful,' but not 'vicious.' "

"Does it bother you?" Chiun asked. There was the hint of a smile on his calm Oriental face.

"No," Remo said.

The hint of a smile vanished. "I will think of something else," Chiun promised.

"I'm sure you will," Remo said. " 'Vicious heart' is going to be hard to top, though."

Chiun, of course, had not killed the salesman. Oh, no. He made that clear. He had merely attempted to become part of the computer age. Through the centuries that the House of Sinanju had worked for emperors and rulers, tributes had piled up at the small village on the West Korean Bay. Gifts from the Greekling, Alexander, from pharaohs and kings, from all who had wished to employ the ancient Korean house of assassins. Gifts too numerous to list. Computers were good at listing such things and so Chiun, who liked the gadgets of the West, called a salesman and purchased a computer, one that could do lists well.

The salesman had arrived that day, bearing a lovely machine, finely tooled, with a beautiful gray box to house it and a keyboard of glistening keys.

Chiun explained the problems of listing different weights, because the ancient Masters would get paid in weights of stone, and also in dramits, pulons and refids, such as a major refid of silk or a minor refid of silk.

"No problem," the salesman had said. "How big is a refid? I'll just put it right in the computer."

"It depends on the quality of the silk," Chiun had said. "A small refid of fine silk is better than a large refid of poor silk. It is both quantity and quality."

"I see. So a refid means value."

"Yes," Chiun said.

"No problem," the salesman said. "How much is a single refid worth in money?"

"One refid?" asked Chiun.

"Sure," said the salesman pleasantly.

"A single refid is equal to three and seven-eights barons during the time of the Ming Dynasty, or one thousand, two hundred and twelve Herodian shekels from that fine king of Judea."

It had taken the whole morning but the salesman had studiously set up a value system for the many different weights and measures of the House of Sinanju. Chiun's fingers fluttered expectantly as he waited for the moment when he himself could touch the keys and record, for the first time in centuries, all the glorious tributes of the House of Sinanju. For this meant in centuries to come, every Master to follow would have to think of Chiun when they examined the wealth that would be passed on to them.

"Can we put my name on every page?" Chiun asked.

"Sure," said the salesman, and he programmed every page to list automatically and forever that this accounting had been started by Chiun. They could even make the pages shorter so that Chiun's name would appear more often.

"Should we say 'the Great Chiun'?" Chiun asked.

"Sure," said the salesman again, and he inserted it into the program. Such was Chiun's happiness that tears almost came to his eyes.

The old Korean sat before the keyboard and touched it with his fingers. Then he began to list the modern tributes sent by submarine from the new nation of America to Korea as payment for "the Great Chiun's" teaching services.

He paused, imagining future generations reading this. They would tell stories of him, just as he, as a student, had been told stories of the Great Wang and other past Masters of Sinanju. He had told Remo the stories so that the young white man would understand what it was to be a Master of Sinanju.

And then, as Chiun pressed the precious keys again, a dull gray mass appeared suddenly on the screen and all the letters were gone.

"Where is my name?" he asked.

"Oh, you hit the delete-key format instead of the file-key format," the salesman said.

"Where is my name?"

"If we had made a backup disk, your name would still be there. But we didn't. So, in the future, you're going to have to make a backup disk, do you see?"

"Where is my name?" asked Chiun.

"It was deleted."

"My name was in there forever. That is what you said."

"Yes. It was."

"Forever," Chiun explained, "does not have a 'was'." Forever is always an 'is.' Where is my name?"

"You struck the delete-key format."

"Where is my name?"

"It's not there."

"I put it there and you put it there," Chiun said. "You said it was there forever. Bring it back."

"We can always reenter your name," the salesman said.

At that point, realizing he was dealing with someone of little understanding, Chiun in his fairness made an offer to the salesman. If he would bring back Chiun's name, Chiun would buy the computer.

"We can always reenter it," the salesman said. "But the old name's gone forever." He chuckled. "Names come and names go. Just like people. Heh, heh. Come and go."

And thus it was that the salesman went. He had reached for the plug to disconnect the computer and Chiun, of course, could not let the computer that had failed leave with his name in it.

That was the first unpleasantness of the day. The second was Remo's return, jumping to a conclusion that Chiun had somehow created a body for him to dispose of. Chiun hadn't created anything. He had suffered because of a computer that did not work. Chiun had suffered from having his name deleted. And the salesman had suffered from having his existence deleted. Having unintentionally hit one delete-key format, Chiun had hit another, the one located above the salesman's ear, at his temple, driving in a fingernail for a permanent delete.

"I don't suppose you want to know what that man did to my name," said Chiun.

"I don't care," Remo said. "He's your body, not mine."

"I didn't think you would care for the truth," Chiun said. "After all, you don't care what happens to the glory of the House of Sinanju and you never have."

"I'm not disposing of the body," said Remo.

"Well, neither am I," said Chiun.

Both of them heard the footsteps outside, the halting steps of a man whose unenlightened body was deteriorating in the common Western manner of old age.

"Smith called. He will be here this afternoon," Chiun said.

"This is the afternoon," Remo said.

"And here he is," Chiun said. An elderly man, his face gaunt, his thinning hair white, walked up the creaky steps and knocked at the door.

Remo answered it.

"How did it go today?" asked Smith. "Did you get the hard disk and the backups?"

"Hard disk and backups," said Remo. "Right. They've been taken care of."

He shut the door behind Smith. Remo only knew that he had stayed young by noticing how old Smith had gotten during their years together, how the man's movements became restricted, how his steps had started their dissipation toward an inevitable shuffle.

Remo wondered sometimes if this was because Smith had never learned to use his body properly or if it was the tension of his work that was crippling him. For almost twenty-five years, Smith had headed CURE, the secret agency whose mission was to fight America's enemies, inside or outside the law. Remo was the organization's killing arm, and it was his activities that the two unlucky computer executives had stumbled onto.

Remo decided to make Smith feel better. "Everything's been taken care of," he said. "But you ought to get a new system for your computers. Everybody seems able to break into them these days."

"We're taking care of that," Smith said, sinking gingerly into a chair. "We have, thank God, discovered a genius who'll set us up in such a way that you won't have to terminate any more poor souls who stumble onto our files. But we have other important problems facing us now."

"We stand ready to serve, Emperor Smith," said Chiun. He refused to call the head of the secret organization anything but Emperor. Through the ages, Masters of Sinanju had always worked for royalty.

Smith nodded but his face suddenly showed alarm.

"What is that?" he asked Remo, pointing across the room.

"Nothing," Remo said. "It's Chiun's."

"That's a body," Smith said.

"Right," Remo said. "It's Chiun's."

Smith looked at Chiun, who said, "Would you like to purchase a computer?" Then, in Korean, he reminded Remo never to discuss family business in front of Smith.

"We've got to get out of here," Smith said. "We can't be discovered by the police."

"We'll move," Remo said. "It's a fresh body. We've got time."

"I hope the police do come and they can take their foul, evil, deleting computer with them," said Chiun. He turned back to Smith, again smiling. "We commiserate with you and your problems and we are here to give glory to your name."

Smith started to speak but could not take his eyes off the body. Remo and Chiun did not seem to mind it and he thought that perhaps it was the awesome skill with which these assassins worked that had made death cease to have real meaning for them. He did not know, and he realized, sadly, that it didn't matter. He no longer really cared about life and death that much himself.

"So what's this big thing you want us to work on?" Remo said cheerily.

Smith steadied himself and took a great breath of air.

"Remo," he said, "what do you know about insects?"

3

"Not yet, Mr. Perriweather," said the scientist.

"Oh," said Waldron Perriweather III, disappointed.

"Maybe in two weeks, sir."

"Yes, of course. No sooner?"

"I'm afraid not, sir."

Perriweather sighed and took one more look into the microscope.

"We need two more generations, sir. At least," the scientist said.

"I see," said Perriweather. He was feeling dizzy. A sense of breathing difficulty filled his chest. There was that smell again, the one that always sent waves of nausea and fear through his body.

The biologist was working with DDT again. Of course he had to. Perriweather walked past a window that allowed in only dim light through its fine mesh cover. Not even a fly's egg could fit through the glistening nylon mesh. Outside was air, good clean air. Perriweather threw two hands at the window and shoved.

"No," screamed the scientist, diving at Perriweather and pulling him from the window. "What are you doing? Are you crazy?"

"I need air."

"Use the door," said the scientist. He helped his employer to his feet and dragged him toward the door.

Outside the lab door, Perriweather leaned against a marble table imported from a czarist court. The biologist was surprised at how quickly Perriweather recovered.

"I thought you were having a heart attack," he said.

"No. It was the DDT."

"There isn't enough in that room to harm a mouse," said the scientist. "It's amazing. I've never seen anybody as sensitive to it as you are. But you know I have to use it in this stage of the project. You understand that?"

"I do," Perriweather said.

"There's going to be more DDT and other toxins in this lab before we're through. That's if you want this carried out correctly."

"I understand," Perriweather said. "You keep at it."

"But one thing I will not go along with, can't go along with, is your ever opening a window in there," the scientist said. "They must be sealed."

"Go ahead with your work. I understand," Perriweather said.

"And once we achieve success, of course, we must put all our data into files and then destroy what we have created."

Waldron Perriweather III shivered at the thought, but inwardly. He hid it well.

"Of course," he said. He had to say that. The scientist would never have agreed to the project in the first place if Perriweather had not promised to destroy what was created.

But he knew that the time would come when he would not need the biologist, and then, thought

Perriweather, I will happily eat the rotting eyes out of
your ugly head.

He said, with a buzzing little smile, "You're doing a
wonderful job."

And then he was off for another press interview.
The Species Liberation Alliance had struck again.

The parents of a family of five had been strangled.

Apparently they had not been the primary targets.
The SLA had tried to gain access to a laboratory of the
International Health Organization. Police had chased
them until they had them trapped in a nearby
farmhouse where they held the parents as hostages.
They had delivered ten nonnegotiable demands to the
police and when the demands weren't met, killed the
farmer and his wife, while the children looked on.

Then they tried to shoot their way out through a
police barricade. They wounded several state troopers
but were stopped before they could hurl the con-
cussion grenades they had been carrying. State police
bullets nailed them in the front seat of the dead
farmer's car.

It was to this issue that Waldron Perriweather III
addressed himself. The television reporter was sure
that this time he had Perriweather.

"I understand your position as America's leading
spokesman for wildlife preservation," the reporter had
said. "But how on earth can you defend, even
remotely, the murder of parents in front of their
children? People who didn't want anything but to live.
They weren't polluting the atmosphere. As a matter of
fact, the SLA murdered an organic farmer. He didn't
even use pesticides. What do you say to that?"

Perriweather's smooth face appeared as unruffled as
if his eyes had alighted on a large chocolate cake.

"I would like here and now to protest the use of

automatic weapons by the state police. It was an excessive display of force, considering that the SLA used only small revolvers. Where is this country going when police feel free to fire automatic weapons at civilians?"

"They were murderers," the reporter said.

"Who found them guilty? Did they have a trial by jury? No. Their judge and jury was the barrel of an M-16. And what were they trying to do, these two who never had a chance for a fair trial? They were trying to say: 'Look. We are not the only ones on earth. Live and let live. We are not the only creatures in the world.' And for that, they fell, before extraordinary force."

"What about the farmer and his wife? What about the children who are now orphans? What about the police who were wounded?"

"To eradicate so-called terrorism, you must deal with its causes. You will never stop the just and legitimate aspirations of those who care for a just and legitimate new order for all creatures, not only those with the power to get themselves represented and heard, but the powerless also, those creatures who are considered unworthy of living by those who deal death in DDT and other killer toxins."

What bothered the reporter most was that this malicious absurdity would probably be supported on college campuses around the country. The police were going to be put on trial in the media, after stopping two murderers from killing again.

In Washington, the chief of a special FBI detail that had been assigned to protect the laboratories of the International Health, Agricultural and Educational Organization, watched the interview with Perriweather in helpless fury. Hours before, he had been told that his bureau was being relieved of its reponsibility to protect the IHAEO lab.

"We had terrorists attack the lab today. They didn't get in because we were there," said the unit chief. "So why are we being relieved?"

"Orders," he was told by the supervisor, who had a corner office in the J. Edgar Hoover Building.

"But that's ridiculous. We stopped them. That's why they went at the farmer and his family. We prevented them from entering the lab. Us. No other nation has been able to do that."

"I know," said the supervisor. "But orders are orders. Your unit's relieved."

The IHAEO lab had been one of the great intelligence mysteries of the last decade. It was one of the few actually productive parts of the IHAEO, doing international research against crop-destroying insects. Yet the lab was the only part of the IHAEO that had ever been attacked.

This was doubly strange because the lab was the single element of the IHAEO that all nations, rich and poor, communist and capitalist, supported. In fact, the lab had represented what everyone admitted was the only absolutely unassailable good work ever done by the IHAEO.

But over the past decade, the lab had come under repeated physical attack. Scientists were kidnapped, killed, threatened, mutilated and bombed. From one country to another, no matter where the laboratory had been established, scientists were targets.

Secretly, the security forces of many nations had begun what had been their most cooperative effort ever. The lab had started in Ubanga, a developing African country whose major crops suffered vast insect damage. But when IHAEO scientists started to disappear in the crocodile-infested waters, Ubanga swallowed its pride and admitted it could no longer protect the guest scientists. Reluctantly it gave up its host-nation status to Great Britain. The British assigned their crack SAS teams to protect the researchers, under a network especially labeled MI-26.

Within four days after the move to England, a toxin expert was found near the hearth in his new Sussex home with his eyes shot out. After another such incident, the British swallowed their pride, and asked the French to take over. The lab moved to Paris, where, even before the centrifuges could be plugged in, the whole place went up in flames.

At the request of all its members, the lab was moved to the most efficient police state in the world. It was set up in the heart of Moscow and given to the KGB to protect for all mankind.

With constant surveillance and the right to arrest anyone who came anywhere near the lab, the KGB was able to keep the scientists safe, albeit unhappy. For three months. And then a botanist was found clawed to death inside a locked room.

The Russians turned the laboratory over to the United States, and the FBI, using the world's most advanced technology, had kept it safe for four months. Even today, when it had repelled the SLA attack.

And yet the FBI was being relieved of the job and the unit chief wanted to know why. The terrorists hadn't gotten through the final beam barrier and the scientists were still alive. All of them. There was even a lead now on who might be behind the mysterious assaults against the researchers. So why was the FBI being removed? The unit chief demanded to know.

"I'm just following orders. This comes from the highest."

"The director has gone crazy then," the unit chief said.

"Higher," said the supervisor.

"Then the attorney general has gone wacky too."

"The AG doesn't agree with the decision either," the supervisor said.

The unit chief was about to curse political decisions when he suddenly realized that it didn't make sense. Obviously someone close to the President, or even the President himself, had made this decision. But if it had been made for political motives, it was a mistake. Even the White House could have seen that. Here was America accomplishing something that no other nation had been able to do. That lesson wouldn't have been lost on the world, and the White House had to know that. But still the FBI unit was being called off.

The unit chief was almost tempted to give the story to the press. Almost. But he had served loyally for too many years and he distrusted a press that could go into a situation, create disasters and then, as if free of guilt or responsibility, go on with the same exhortations that had created the disasters in the first place.

He contented himself with saying, "It's crazy."

"They're orders," replied his supervisor. "We did a good job. Nobody can take that away from us and we will continue to investigate the SLA. I think there's something bigger behind this thing and I hope someone will get them."

"We stopped an attack. Why were we taken off?"

"I guess someone else is going to take over our job," the supervisor said.

"Great. Who? I'll pass on what we know."

"I have no idea."

"CIA?"

"No," the supervisor said. "Since Peanut Brain,

they'll never be allowed to work inside America again."

"Then who?"

"Nobody knows. And I mean nobody," said the supervisor.

"If it's not us and not the CIA and it wasn't the KGB or the Deuxieme or MI-26, then in God's name, who?"

"Welcome to IHAEO labs, Washington," said Dara Worthington. She wondered whether she dared make friends with these two. She had lost so many friends at IHAEO already. At first she thought that she would show them to their private lab and then flee. But the edlerly man was so sweet and gentle that she just had to say something about the adorable shining green kimono he wore.

"It's beautiful," she said.

"You gotta start that stuff?" said the Oriental's white partner cruelly. His name was Remo. He was incredibly sexy, the kind of man she dreamed of bedding, but he had a rude personality that she didn't care for. It was a detached coldness, a casual lack of caring. When she had greeted him with a warm hello, he had ignored her. She didn't need that. She knew she was beautiful, with glorious red hair and a body many men had told her they would die for. Not that she wanted anyone dead. There had been too much of that around these labs already. But at least when she gave someone a big warm hello, she should get something back, like a little interest.

"Just show us the lab and the other researchers," the one called Remo had said. She ignored him and talked to the elderly Oriental who was so pleasant.

"And don't lose anything of his in a computer," Remo told her.

"Does he always talk to you like that?" Dara had asked.

"It's all right," said Chiun. He was not only sweet and understanding, thought Dara, but he had a nice name too.

"I'm serious about not playing with his computer," Remo said loudly.

"A computer caused me a problem," Chiun told her. "Since then I have been blamed for its failure."

"That doesn't sound fair," Dara said.

"We have worked together for many years now, I and this white thing," the Oriental said sadly. "I do not seek fairness anymore."

"Just don't play with his computer," Remo said, "or you'll really see unfairness."

"You don't have to be so rude," Dara told him.

"Yes, I do," Remo said.

"Why?"

"Because if I weren't rude, you might play with his computer."

Dara let that go but she couldn't let Remo criticize the old man for accepting a compliment on his beautiful kimono.

"I have known you two for just a few minutes, but frankly, I will be blunt," she said.

"Don't bother," Remo said.

"I will. I intend to," she said.

"I thought so," Remo said.

"I don't know why this lovely man puts up with you," she said.

"Are you through?" Remo asked.

"Yes."

"Good. Now show us the lab."

"We learn to live with these things," Chiun told her sadly. "Do you know I have to take out the garbage myself?"

"That's awful," Dara said. "At least he might show some respect."

"You are young and beautiful," said Chiun, "and wise beyond your years."

"That's very touching," she said.

"Where's the lab?" Remo asked.

"Go find it yourself," she snapped.

"Please," said Chiun. "We must understand and bear with the rude and the ungrateful. That is the price of wisdom."

"Little Father, do you want to tell her what the garbage was that I refused to take out?" Remo asked Chiun.

"He's your father and you treat him this way?" asked Dara Worthington, shocked.

"I am his father, not by blood, but by my efforts in trying to teach him the good ways."

Dara understood that. The old man was so beautiful. As they walked past the security devices that now protected every laboratory in the complex, Chiun told her how he had given so much to the younger man who appreciated nothing. Dara thought that Remo was very much like all the men in her life.

She glanced at Remo but he was ignoring her again. He was truly interested in the laboratory complex because when Smith had given them this assignment, the CURE director had seemed genuinely despairing.

It was not fear, just a quiet desperation. Remo had seen it in men's eyes before. They knew death was coming and their motions became not faster, but slower. Even their thinking seemed to tail off as if they did not want to spend energy on a life that was already lost. Smith had acted that way. He seemed to be a man who was watching his world die around him and Remo had picked up his sense of danger, the numb uselessness of despair. That made Smith appear aged.

"Where is Dr. Ravits' lab?" Remo asked Dara.

"It's the one you and your father will be in," said Dara. "You have to pass through extra doors to get to it. The FBI wouldn't even let the doctor leave the lab, so I guess you two won't be able to either."

"The FBI kept him a prisoner?" Remo said.

"You don't know Dr. Ravits," said Dara, cutting off the conversation with a cold smile.

But Remo did know Dr. Ravits. He knew when he was born, when and where he went to school, and how he became an entomologist. He also knew the successes and failures of his career.

Smith had told Remo everything when he came to the oceanfront cottage to give him and Chiun their new assignment. As Smith had explained:

There was a beetle that traditionally had fed on the crops of three tribes in central Africa. The beetle lived in cycles as it had for tens of thousands of years, reproducing rapidly and destroying the crops. When the crops dwindled too much, some chemical reaction would take place in the beetle, telling it to decrease because there was not enough food to support its numbers. Relieved of the pressure from the beetles, the crops rebounded and increased and for a few years the tribes fed well. But then the beetles received the signal to multiply, as if they had sensed the greater amount of food available, and the plague would again hit.

Man and insect had lived like this for thousands of years. Then, suddenly, the beetles did not decrease as they should. The IHAEO began to study the creature. If they could find the chemical signals that made it stop reproducing, they could stop the new plague, and keep the beetle population in check forever.

But then came the horror, Smith had told Remo and Chiun. The real nightmare. For every change the IHAEO scientists made in the Ung beetle, the insect made a counterchange. It became a biological chess game with move and countermove, and the most horrifying thing was that the insects' moves came quickly, within three generations, which was only a matter of months. It was an adaptability to man's attacks that man had never seen before in an insect.

Smith had said, "The one saving grace about this disaster is that the Ung beetle is confined to Central Africa. But given its resistant quality, and its speed of adaptability to other insects, mankind all over the world could literally be deprived of crops. That means we could all starve to death. The tragedy of Central Africa would be the world's tragedy. So now you know why the work of the IHAEO is so important."

"I still don't know what you want me for," Remo had said. "Get a bug doctor."

"Entomologist," Smith said. "We have them. And we are losing them."

"Who'd want to kill a bug doctor?" Remo asked.

"Entomologist," Smith said.

"Right. That."

"We don't know. But someone is. Despite protection around the world, someone is getting to the scientists. It's as if mankind has only one life raft and some lunatics are trying to punch holes in it."

Despite the odds, Smith had explained, mankind might still win. A Dr. Ravits had developed a biochemical substance called a pheromone. It attracted the beetles to each other, but its side effects overcame the beetles' adaptability and made their own defenses work against them.

Chiun, who had been staring angrily at the body behind the computer, entered the conversation. In Korean, he told Remo: "Do not ask Emperor Smith what he is talking about lest he explain it."

In English, Chiun said to Smith: "How fascinating,
O wise emperor."

"I won't go into what a polypusside is," said Smith.

"As you will, O gracious emperor," Chiun said.

"What we want is for you to get into the lab and
whenever they strike again, go after him. So far,
they've gotten through every government's defense
system and we still don't know who they are. This Dr.
Ravits says the pheromone is about ready to go. It has
to be protected."

"They were attacked today," Remo said, "but the
lab people escaped, right?"

"Yes," Smith said. "The FBI has been able to protect
them so far. This might strike you as strange, but that's
precisely because the defense has been successful so far
in America that we feel now is the time to change it."

Chiun almost blinked in surprise. In Korean he let
out, "They are finally thinking."

"Yes," said Remo. He understood. There had never
been a wall that was successful over a long period of
time. Even the brilliantly designed tombs of the
Egyptian pharaohs had, over the centuries, given up
their treasures to robbers. The world always changed
and he who sought to survive had to change also,
before it was too late. It was why Chiun had tried to
buy a computer.

"It's a good idea, Smitty," Remo told Smith. "You
relax now and leave it to us." He tried to smile. "It's
taken too long for me to break you in. I don't want to
work with anyone else."

"I'm afraid someday you will have to. I'm getting
too old and you don't seem to be," Smith said.

"Oh no, gracious emperor," Chiun said. "You are
like the flower that blooms more beautifully as the
days go on."

"You are most kind, Master of Sinanju," said Smith.

And in Korean, Chiun muttered when Smith left: "See, Remo, what happens when you eat the wrong meat. See? Leaving now on those shuffling feet is a hamburger eater."

"I guess so," said Remo unenthusiastically. But he felt for Smith; he felt for someone who cared about the things Remo still cared about. The world was worth saving, especially the part of it Remo loved: the United States.

"I guess," Remo repeated sadly. He was going to do this assignment for Smith because it might just be the old man's last, and so he and Chiun went on ahead to the IHAEO labs and met Dara Worthington.

Now they followed her into Dr. Ravits' laboratory.

Ravits was looking at a computer printout as he chewed great mouthfuls of chocolate cake and drank a glass of sugared soda with caffeine additives. His face looked like a World War I battlefield with craters left by triumphant acne.

His hands shook and his white lab coat was dirty. Dr. Ravits apparently did not believe strongly in changing clothes or bathing.

In the hallway, Dara Worthington had warned Remo and Chiun that Ravits simply lost contact with anything that wasn't connected with his work. He was not basically a slob, just a person engaged in work so consuming that he didn't have time for the rest of the world. He tended to eat cake and soda because he never quite remembered to eat a meal. Once, when they had been in Russia, Dara had brought him a warm meal on a platter and forced him to eat.

"Have some salad," she had said.

"Will you marry me?" Ravits had said.

"I only said have some salad."

"You are the most meaningful relationship I've had in my life."

"I'm the only one and all I did was tell you to eat."

"Then you won't marry me?" he said.

"No," said Dara.

"Then would you empty the wastebaskets, please,"
Dr. Ravits had said. "They're getting full."

Ravits looked up from the printout as she brought
Remo and Chiun into the lab.

"These two entomologists are here to assist you, Dr.
Ravits," she said. She seemed to thrust forward,
stretching her bosom against her prim white blouse.
The laboratory smelled as though it had housed an
electrical fire for the last month. Remo realized it was
Ravits.

"Good," said Ravits. He nodded at Remo and
Chiun. "I think you two ought to know we have lost
several people from this lab to terrorists, yes?"

"We know," said Remo.

"I'll leave you three together," said Dara, bowing
out. "Dr. Ravits, you ought to get along very well with
Dr. Chiun. I found him most pleasant."

Remo ignored the insult. He glanced at the windows
and noticed the very small sensing devices that would
set off alarms. The glass was thick enough to bounce
back a howitzer shell. The air conditioning did not
bring in outside air, which might be poisoned, but
recirculated the old air with infusions of oxygen, and
other elements removed.

It looked safe enough. A black cat with white paws
purred contentedly next to a small heater in the
corner.

"That's my best friend," Ravits said. "Cats are
wonderful pets. They leave you alone." Ravits smiled
once as if imitating an expression he once saw in a
photograph and went back to his computer readout.

"Is there a phone in here?" Remo asked.

"There should be. I guess so. I don't use it. Nobody I want to call. Do you always talk so much?"

"We're etymologists," said Chiun, folding his long fingernails into his kimono. He pronounced the syllables of the word very slowly.

"Then what are you doing here?" said Ravits. "Etymology is the study of words."

"The other one," Remo said.

"Entomologists?" Ravits asked.

"Right," said Remo. "That."

"Makes sense. That's why you're with me," Ravits said and put his soul back into the reproductive habits of the Ung beetle.

Remo found the telephone in the corner. He dialed the number Smith had given him. It didn't work. He often got the code numbers wrong, but this one Smith had written down.

He dialed again but it still didn't answer. He would have to go outside to telephone. Ravits did not know where the nearest outside phone was. The smell from his body reeked through the small lab.

"You stay here and I'll check in with Smitty," Remo told Chiun.

"I will stand on the outside of the door where the air is better," Chiun said.

Remo found a working phone in the lab office next to Ravits'. Chiun waited outside by the only entrance and everything else was sealed. Ravits was safe.

This telephone worked.

"Yes?" Smith's voice clicked.

"Just wanted to let you know that everything is fine." Remo said.

"Good."

"He's in a room with only one entrance and Chiun is standing there."

"Good," said Smith.

"We'll just wait for them to attack."

"Good," said Smith.

"How does Long Island Sound look?" Remo asked.

"I'm not at Folcroft," Smith said.

"In the Islands?" Remo asked.

"St. Martin. The computer backup area," Smith said.

"Good. Enjoy the weather," Remo said. "Listen, Smitty, don't worry, all right?"

"All right," Smith said.

Remo hung up the telephone and walked out to the fluorescent-lit hallway, so welded with steel that it looked like the inside of a submarine.

"We'll just wait," Remo told Chiun. He felt good about having been able to reassure Smith.

"Not inside," Chiun said. "I will not wait in there."

"Inside," said Remo.

"You wait inside," Chiun said. "I will wait here."

Remo opened the door to the lab. The computer printout that Ravits had been poring over was now red and glistening. A pile of what looked like butcher's garbage rested on the paper. A pale shard of pinkish skin caught Remo's eye. The skin had acne.

The pile was what was left of Dr. Ravits.

4

The problem was solved.

Finally, after years of ad hoc plugging of ad hoc gaps, the security problems with CURE's computers were solved.

Dr. Harold W. Smith walked out onto the white sandy beach of the perfect Caribbean bay of Grand Case on the French side of the Antilles island of St. Martin. He would get some sun. He had done a good job.

He felt that if he died now, in his last moment he could look back on his life and say he had done a good job for his country and even for the human race.

He had been pleased by Remo's phone call, too. Smith had been worried because it had been a risk to lift the FBI protection that had been working so well, but it would have been a greater risk to leave it the way it was.

Nobody could have blamed him if he had ignored the danger and left things along. But it was precisely because he had never tried to enhance his career that he had been chosen, many years ago, by a now-dead President, to run the new organization to fight America's enemies.

No, Smith thought, he had only done what he had

to do. The real courage had been shown by the President. Smith had asked for an urgent meeting. Because of the nature of CURE, the meeting had to be kept secret even from the President's staff, and that could be sticky. The problem, even with trusted staff members, was that the more trusted they were, the more they felt they had to know everything. And that was how information got leaked, by too many people knowing it. Smith explained that they had to meet away from the President's staff.

"How?" the President asked. "Do I send them away?"

"No, Mr. President," Smith had said. "You leave them at the center of things. You see, their interest goes up when they feel left out of things. So you go on vacation, sir. Go to your ranch in California and then talk to the new assistant gardener."

"You want me to have you put on the ranch payroll?"

"I want you to have no contact with me, sir."

"You can't get on the ranch payroll without being checked out," the President said, then paused. "Oh, I forgot. You control some of the people who do the checking out, don't you?"

Harold Smith did not answer that. He did not control the people who investigated the information on his employment application; he controlled the information itself. Everything worked on computers, and CURE had been using them even before the Defense Department. CURE had always been ahead of the rest of the world, which was how it had been able to function with so few knowing of its existence. And a computer had no compulsion to share information with a best friend.

CURE lived and died by these computers. It took only a simple pushing of a few keys to give Harold W.

Smith his clearance to be an assistant gardener at the President's California ranch, after first telling the ranch's head gardener that he needed an assistant.

So when the President flew to California for a brief rest, the first thing he did was examine the rosebushes along the stockade-style fence.

An elderly gardener was clipping around the thorns. The President sidled over to him and for all the world looked as if he were discussing rosebushes with him because every once in a while the gardener would gesticulate with his pruning shears. But the conversation went like this:

"Mr. President, I am going to ask you to take a risk that on its face might not seem logical."

"Go ahead. Try me," the President said with his usual good humor.

"You're familiar with the International Health, Agricultural and Educational Organization?"

"Sure. The thing with four thousand overpaid people who make a profession out of attacking America with America's money."

"I'm talking about their entomology labs."

"The one part of the whole shebang that works. And someone is trying to kill them. I've seen the reports and I've got the FBI protecting the lab. They're doing it well, too. Even the KGB couldn't handle it."

"I'm asking you to call off the FBI and let us take care of it."

"Why?"

"Because sooner or later, the FBI won't be able to protect them," Smith said, and explained the dangers that the labs were fighting. The only real defense would be to get at the people who were killing the scientists. The FBI couldn't do that and, no matter how good the defense, eventually the labs would be penetrated.

The President looked puzzled. "Why can't we leave the FBI where it is and just go after the crazies, whoever they are?"

"Because then they'll delay attacking. But it'll still happen eventually and we have to prevent that," Smith said.

"Are you going to use those people?" the President asked, referring to the two men who seemed to be able to penetrate anything at will, including the White House. He had seen them operate once and immediately wanted to know if America could get more of them. He had looked sad when Smith said there were only two in the world like that.

Smith nodded and the President said, "Do you know what will happen if someone else is killed and it comes out that I ordered the defenses away?"

"I think so," Smith said.

"I've got a press that would love to hang me. This time they wouldn't have to make up anything."

"I know that."

"How sure are you that your plan will work?" the President asked.

"I know this. If we go on the way we're going, they'll strike again. They're incredibly clever and seem to be able to penetrate anything when they want. How they got into Russia, I'll never know."

"So you want me to stick my neck out?"

"Yes, sir," said Smith. "Only your direct orders can get the FBI out of the way."

"How bad is this bug business?" the President wanted to know.

"It could be all the marbles, Mr. President. Right now, the problem areas are in the Third World but it could spread." Harold W. Smith clipped another twig of the rosebush, absentmindedly trying to remember whether he was supposed to clip above or below a main stem. It didn't matter. He would be gone by nightfall.

"Why don't we just put our own scientists on the damned thing and forget the IHAEO?" the President asked.

"They have most of the good entomologists," Smith said.

The President thought for a moment while Smith mutilated another rosebush. Then the President slowly nodded.

"Don't let me down," he said. His voice was low and he moved off along the fence as if out for an afternoon stroll. Three hours later, the new assistant gardener was gone for good.

Smith remembered the afternoon. He felt an obligation to a man who had done the right thing. It would work. More and more through the years, he had understood Remo less and less and he had never understood Chiun. But this was the sort of thing they were good at, and now Remo had reported that things were under control. Dr. Ravits was safe.

And to make matters better in the St. Martin sun, he had solved the computer problems forever. He felt good. He rubbed in the suntan cream to protect his pale skin from the sun's intense heat. He could even believe now that he was lucky. He had never believed in luck before, but now he had to say, after so many years of grinding calculation, that yes, he was quite lucky.

Suddenly, someone was tapping him on the shoulder and Smith looked up to see the black bell-bottoms of a gendarme. The policeman wore a pistol in a black holster. His blue shirt bore the insignia of the French national police.

"Are you Harold W. Smith?" he asked with a thick accent.

"Yes," said Smith.

"Would you come with me, sir?" the gendarme said. The tone of his voice told Smith nothing but Smith knew that the gendarmes were quite polite because of the island's tourist business. They would rarely ticket a car no matter how it was parked, and they had their own special sort of justice.

Recently, when a tourist's wife had been raped, they brought the suspect to the woman's husband, an American policeman, and left them alone for five minutes. They they deported what remained of the suspect to another island. There was no long, drawn-out trial.

Many things were done like that, and that gave CURE exactly what it needed most: a place without a very inquisitive local police force. Justice and law enforcement were rather basic in St. Martin and, since computers never threatened anyone, the organization could be sure to be left alone on a quiet island in a rolling sea.

"May I ask why I must go with you?" Smith said.

"You must accompany me to Marigot," the gendarme said.

Smith reasoned he was being taken to police head-quarters since Marigot was the capital of the French half of the island. "May I put on something more than a bathing suit?"

"But of course," said the gendarme.

Ordinarily Smith might have been concerned at this point, but with the computers now safe from any invasions, he actually whistled as he went into the apartment facing the beach. He rented the apartment from the man who supplied the entire island with gasoline, a franchise the man's family had owned for several generations.

Smith wriggled out of his bathing suit while the

policeman waited politely outside the apartment. He took a short shower to get rid of the sand, and then put on a pair of shorts, a T-shirt and sandals. He also took the key to the solution of all the organization's computer programs.

It was the size of an attaché case and it held more memory capability than all the computers the Strategic Air Command had secreted in the Rocky Mountains. The truth was that CURE no longer needed its offices at Folcroft Sanitarium in Rye, New York, just as it no longer needed the offices which were carved out of the coral hills behind the salt flats in Grand Case. All it needed was the briefcase in Smith's hand. For what Smith had finally done was to find one genius who had discovered a source of memory almost as infinite as space.

It went beyond bubble technology. It used the cosmic relationships between stars. The very energy that would attract light now stored the information from throughout the world in a single access disk.

"You see," the computer genius had said, "you don't need to store memory, you only need to access it, to reach it. Well, that means you can use anything to store it if you want, even light refraction. Do you understand?"

"Frankly, no," Smith had said.

"You don't have to. It works," Barry Schweid had said. And it did.

Schweid was twenty-five, lived at home with his mother, and spent eighteen hours a day over a small personal computer which he said he had "juiced up." He didn't really care that much after salary. His mother did, however, and she also worried about him meeting nice girls, eating properly and getting sun. She wouldn't let Barry out of the house unless nice Mr. Smith, his new employer, promised he would get at least two hours of fresh air a day and that Barry would eat at least one good healthy meal a day.

Those promises given, Schweid had come to work for Smith, who sent him to St. Martin, where CURE kept up a big bank of computers that duplicated all the information in the computers at CURE's main head-quarters in Folcroft Sanitarium.

"I want you to make our computer files entry-proof," Smith had said.

And Schweid had.

Basically what he had done was to take all CURE's information and devise a new way to make it available through the equipment that fit into the attaché case.

"How does that help?" Smith had asked. "Now I've got three sets of files that can be entered instead of two."

"No," Schweid had said. "You don't understand."

"No, I don't."

"Here it is. What this allows us to do is to put a trap net on the other computers, the ones at Folcroft and here."

"What will that do?"

"It will allow us to jigger those other computers so that if anybody breaks into them, in any way, the computers will simply erase themselves. Totally."

"Everything will be gone?"

"Right. Before anybody can steal it. And because you've got the master file in that attaché case, you can always refill the main computers at some later date if you want."

The only problem was getting access through the attaché-case computer. Schweid was still needed for that because of its intricacy, but he had promised Smith that he would soon deliver a modified access system which would allow Smith to get into the files himself without Schweid's help.

This had brought a rare, unaccustomed smile to Smith's face. The world was working well. He was getting rest in St. Martin, the world's problems seemed to be under control, and he even surprised his own lemony critical nature by not worrying about why the gendarme had come to pick him up.

He picked up the attaché case that he had purposely made to look old and beat up, something that might be carrying dirty laundry rather than access to the world's greatest collection of evil secrets.

Harold W. Smith's nature was that he could wear checkered Bermuda shorts and a yellow T-shirt and look perfectly natural carrying an attaché case. He always looked as if he should have some sort of briefcase, even when he slept.

Downstairs, the small Citroën police car sat in the dusty alley between the white beachfront homes. The gendarme opened the door for Smith. Unlike American police cars, there was no protective screen between driver and passengers. The only thing that made this bouncy little Citroën a police car was a reflective light on top and a French-national-police label on the side, the symbol of a torch.

As they pulled out into the streets of Grand Case, so narrow that one car had to pull over onto the curb whenever a vehicle came in the opposite direction, the gendarme asked very casually the one question that could send Smith into shock.

"Pardon, sir. Do you know a Barry Schweid?"

"Is he all right?" Smith asked.

"Somewhat," the gendarme said.

"What happened?"

"He gave us your name."

"Yes, I know him. I employ him. I have an import-export business."

"Do you know that he is a dangerous man?"

"Barry?" asked Smith. The boy was as mild as milk. In fact, the only thing a really thorough investigation of Barry's past had revealed was a kindergarten incident where he wet his pants. The boy filed his income taxes on time, once reporting a twenty-dollar bill he had found on the street. He had had five dates in all his life, and on one of those, when the girl had gone into the bedroom to get into something comfortable, Barry had fled, thinking it was a reflection on him and the entire evening. If she were comfortable with him, he reasoned, she ought to have been comfortable in her clothing.

Barry Schweid had been kissed on his twenty-second birthday when friction stopped the spinning motion of a bottle at a party his mother gave for him.

Barry had been seeing a therapist for three years because of his fear of raising his voice. In fact, he had once got to Curaçao because he had been afraid to tell the stewardess that he had blundered onto the wrong plane.

"What on earth has he done?" Smith asked.

"He has violently assaulted a market woman at the docks in Marigot."

"That sounds impossible."

"While she was coming to the aid of a gendarme."

At Rue Charles de Gaulle in the steaming small port city that was the capital of the island's French side, Harold W. Smith spoke to the prefect of the island police.

He assured the prefect that he knew the young man, knew his background intimately, knew the family. It did not hurt that Smith spoke French fluently. In World War II, in the old OSS, he had parachuted into France. While by nature, he never discussed such things, in this case he allowed it to get into the conversation. He also shrewdly let the prefect know that he was saved by the underground and that if it had not been for the French, Smith would have been a dead man.

To hear Smith talk, one would have believed that the French had liberated America during the war and not vice versa. The prefect saw before him that rare American who was a gentleman. He allowed as how the law did not have to be as formidable in the Caribbean as it was in Paris.

Smith offered amends to both the gendarme and the market woman, though he was mystified as to how Barry Schweid could have started a commotion. He offered a thousand francs to the woman and two thousand American dollars to the officer. "For their trouble," he said.

The prefect knowingly put a palm on the back of Smith's hand.

"One thousand American dollars is enough of a salve for his dignity, monsieur," he said with a wink.

And thus justice was done on Rue Charles de Gaulle between two old allies, who embraced warmly. With the money paid, Smith got Barry released. Smith could overhear men in the police headquarters commenting on how they were bringing out "the monster" and everyone should be wary. Sidearms silently came out of holsters. One burly officer gripped a lead-weighted stick.

In the main police room, between two large gendarmes, waddled a frightened, very pale and somewhat pudgy young man whose hair looked as if it hadn't seen a comb since the crib.

Barry still wore a flannel shirt and long pants and was sweating profusely. He had been afraid to go outside in a new country and so had stayed in the air-conditioned apartment, working. Smith had vainly tried to get him outside, saying he had promised Barry's mother the boy would get some sun.

"I will. A little bit later," Barry had said. "But not now." Smith did, however, get Barry to bathe and brush his teeth each day. And he did promise to comb his hair, but somehow his work always seemed more important than the seven seconds hair-combing would take.

Now he stood, five-feet five, semishaven, very meek and quite frightened, between two large French policemen.

"Hello, Barry," said Smith.

"Hello, Harold," said Barry softly.

"Are you all right, Barry?"

"No, Harold."

"What's wrong, Barry?"

Barry Schweid extended a finger and motioned Smith to come closer.

"You want to whisper it, Barry?"

"Yes, Harold."

Smith went over to the young man and asked that the guards move away a bit, then bent down to hear the complaint.

"I see, yes," said Smith. "Who has it?"

"I think him, Harold," said Barry. He nodded to a gendarme behind a large flat desk with the picture of the French premier behind it.

"Just a minute," said Smith and went over to the gendarme, who looked at him suspiciously.

Smith whispered in French.

"Did you take away a piece of soft blue cloth when you arrested Mr. Schweid?"

The gendarme said that he didn't quite remember, just as the prefect entered to make sure his compatriot,

Harold W. Smith of the Second World War, was properly taken care of.

"You want a piece of cloth? Garbage?" asked the prefect.

As soon as he heard the word "garbage," the gendarme at the desk remembered. Schweid had been clinging to a piece of blue cloth when he was arrested and they threw it away.

"Could you get it again?" asked Smith in French.

"It's in the garbage," said the gendarme.

"Shh, not so loud," said Smith.

"What are you all whispering about?" screamed Barry, and three gendarmes drew pistols and aimed them at Barry's chest. Barry collapsed in the corner, covering his head with his arms and screaming.

"Get the cloth, damn it," snapped Smith.

"Go, go," ordered the prefect.

"It's all right, Barry," Smith said. "They're getting it. They're getting it."

But Barry only screamed and kicked his legs uselessly in the air. The computer genius was having a tantrum.

Guns returned to their holsters. Gendarmes exchanged puzzled looks in the station on Rue Charles de Gaulle. The prefect assured his American ally that Schweid had been a most dangerous adversary on the docks. In fact, the market woman who was injured weighed 220 pounds and was perhaps the strongest person on the island, including the Dutch side, where they had many large, uncivilized people.

Smith nodded. He did not know what had happened, but when they got the cloth, he would then be able to talk to Barry and find out. He assured the noble prefect that most certainly the incident would never happen again.

"If Mr. Schweid must commit that sort of mayhem," whispered the prefect, "and we do know a man's nature is his nature after all, there are places for it. There is, after all, the Dutch side of the island. You understand."

Smith nodded but assured the prefect that such violence was not normally in the young man's character. A gendarme came into the station carrying the blue piece of cloth at arm's length and holding his nose. It smelled of fish and rotted fruit and coffee grounds. It had been thrown into the garbage disposal.

"That's it. Mine," yelled Barry.

"It's all right, Barry. We're bringing it to you."

"Thank you, Harold," said Barry, sobbing and gratefully clutching the dirty cloth to his cheek. Barry Schweid, computer genius of the organization's vast secret network and newly named "Monster of Marigot," cried meekly and sucked his thumb.

The prefect gave them a driver to return them north to the village of Grand Case. Instead of going to their apartment, Smith had the driver leave them off at what appeared to be the gravel works on a road to a cul-de-sac. Inside the simple office of the gravel works, behind the mosquito-infested salt flats, Smith led Barry to a rear office which secretly opened up into a large cave that housed the storage and retrieval area of CURE's computer network.

It was here that Schweid had devised the portable system that Smith now carried. He also had figured out a way not only to make Smith's files entry-proof, but to find out the identity of anyone who accidentally came close to tapping into the network. Smith, who was not a neophyte to technology himself, never could figure out how.

When the doors behind them were closed, sealed

beyond penetration by interlocking steel plates, Smith asked the simple question:

"What happened in Marigot?"

"It's all your fault," Barry Schweid said. He was rubbing his ear with a corner of the blanket.

"My fault?" Smith asked. "How?"

"I don't want to tell you."

"Barry, listen. You know we do a lot of work we don't want others to know about. We can't have attention called to ourselves or people will get curious."

"Secret work?" Barry said.

"Yes," Smith said, and Barry nodded. He brushed an old piece of fish from his blanket and stuffed it into his rear pocket.

"Well, all right," he said. "It's these files." He pointed to the large banks of computers that circled the walls of the cave.

"What about them?"

"You entered some old stuff and put your initials on the entries, and I was scanning the files, doing a . . . well, never mind, it was complicated, but this file popped out. And it had your observations on it. You were saying you talked to someone you had recruited and asked what he was doing. And he was saying that he wasn't doing anything except learning how to breathe and the whole thing was stupid and he was going to quit on you anyhow."

Instantly Smith knew what Barry Schweid had discovered. They were Smith's early observations on Remo's training, his very earliest training when Smith had brought in Chiun to try to create a single enforcement arm, one man to do the work that really should have been done by thousands.

Schweid was still talking. "It didn't make sense, of course, if you looked at it for just what people were saying. But it kept popping out because it kept integrating itself into the basic cosmic formulas for power. You understand mass and energy and the speed of light, don't you?"

"As well as most laymen, I guess," said Smith.

"Well, just imagine light curving and you have the whole thing," said Schweid.

Smith cleared his throat. It was beyond anything he could understand.

Barry said, "In the light of cosmic power, the same kind we're using to store all your files now, you can understand what the breathing means. It means synchronizing yourself with these rhythms. Therefore, you're really reflecting the curving of light in its own power. In theory."

"And in practice?" Smith asked.

"Well, I tried it," said Barry, "and suddenly I had all sorts of confidence and I went outside and practically ran all the way to Marigot which has got to be five or six miles and then at the market someone pushed me and I just sort of pushed back."

"Was it that gendarme?" Smith asked.

"Yes, I think so."

"You shattered his collarbone," Smith said.

"Oh, dear."

"And then you threw a 220-pound woman halfway down the street and she is still in the hospital."

"Oh, dear, oh, dear," said Barry. The security blanket came back out of his pocket.

"Could you do these things all the time?" Smith asked.

"What? The breathing thing that gave me the power? No. You see, you have to be able not to think. If you think about what you're doing, you can't do it."

"Like an athletic action," asked Smith, who understood that thinking about a golf swing often ruined it.

"More intensely, though. Everything is quantumed out of sight in this thing."

"Could somebody else learn this?" Smith asked. "Maybe all the time?"

"Possibly, but there really has to be a synch to the max. The odds against it are astronomical."

This surprised Smith because for all he knew, Remo and Chiun always seemed to be in some sort of conflict. There was no apparent synchronization between them.

Or maybe, he thought, it was that Remo and Chiun were both synchronized to something else, to some basic elemental force that each used and no one else could. Chiun had often told Smith that Remo was special, one of a kind. Could it be true? Had Smith just been involved in a miraculous, happy accident when he happened to pick Remo Williams, smart-ass Newark cop, to be CURE's enforcement arm?

He put the entire question out of his mind and decided to keep a promise to Barry's mother.

"Can you get up enough courage to go for a walk with me?" he asked.

"Among strangers?"

"People are all strangers until you get to know them, Barry. I was a stranger to you once myself."

"But Mother said you were a nice man."

"You can bring your blankey," said Smith.

"People will laugh. I know they will."

"Well, then leave Blankey here where it'll be safe," Smith suggested.

"I think I'll take it," said Barry, clutching the blue blanket to his chest. He agreed to walk all the way from the gravel works to Grand Case, almost an entire quarter of a mile.

As they were leaving, there was a slight buzz inside Smith's attaché case. Barry quickly ascertained that a message had been received. It had come while Smith was in the cave with Barry. Barry retrieved the message, which had come from the President of the United States.

It read:

"What have you done to me?"

5

For almost ten years, world news media had ignored the murders and the problems at the IHAEO laboratories. But on this afternoon, there was just a hint of the possibility that the death of Dr. Ravits at IHAEO had been caused by the President of the United States.

So at the presidential press conference, the peace he had arranged between two warring factions in South America was ignored, the new donations of enough grain to feed half of Africa was overlooked, and the upcoming arms negotiation agreement was not even mentioned.

"Could the President of the United States explain why, after successfully protecting the IHAEO laboratory, the FBI was removed?" asked one reporter who had never before in her life said a kind word about the FBI. In fact, she had once called for its abolition, saying it should be replaced by a civilian review board composed of blacks, women and the socially alienated. Her definition of socially alienated was anyone doing fifteen-to-life for homicide.

"I take full responsibility for what happened," the President responded. "Yes, I was the one who ordered the FBI withdrawn. I cannot say anything more but that there are plans under way for permanently securing the safety of the IHAEO project. I might point out that a sitting target, no matter how well defended, cannot be defended forever. And that's all I can say."

For twenty minutes the press banged away on that one topic.

Why change what worked? What was his other plan that he couldn't talk about? How could the press know that he wasn't just hiding behind national security and doing dirty things in the night?

"Look," the President said finally. "I made a decision. Maybe it was the wrong one but I take full responsibility for it."

Immediately, there were half a dozen commentators remarking on how cunning the President was to politically manipulate his way out of the problem by taking responsibility.

One said, "Once again we see a President escaping blame by the absolutely unscrupulous method of appearing honest. How many snafus can he escape with that trick?"

Some columnists even hinted that the President might be behind the killings himself, as a way to eliminate the entire IHAEO.

"Hey, look, fellows," the President explained, "I'm not against the IHAEO labs. I've never been against the labs because they're the only thing that works in the entire IHAEO. What I have against the IHAEO is that they don't have enough labs where real work is done. They have mansions in Paris, London, Rome and Hong Kong, and they have one lab. They have four thousand employees, all of them very well paid, and fewer than fifty scientists. And the scientists *aren't* that well paid."

"Then why would you want to destroy the lab?" asked one television newsman. He had earned his reputation for being a keen journalist by sneaking into a barber shop to examine hair trimmings to see if the President dyed his hair.

The President was still able to chuckle. "Well, if you had listened to my last sentence instead of preparing your loaded question, you'd realize that I am *for*, not against, the labs. I am against corruption. I am against private jets and mansions and against our paying lots of people just to hang around and knock America. I am referring to the last IHAEO resolution that blamed American capitalism for the majority of communicable diseases and which, for some unknown reason, praised the Palestine Liberation Organization for blowing up a Jewish hospital as a way of fighting disease. Now, really. Do you think that that's fighting disease?"

"Mr. President, what do you have against fighting disease?"

The body had been tampered with. It had been shredded and torn, the skeletal structure crushed.

Dr. Ravits' pet cat purred contentedly by the heating unit, its feline loyalty ready to be attached to its next bowl of milk, showing all the sympathy for its dead owner that a tree exhibits for its last leaf in autumn.

Remo sometimes wondered what life would be like for a cat. He understood their nervous system and their sense of balance, but he sometimes wished he could master that utter lack of caring, particularly when caring sometimes hurt so much.

"We lost him," said Remo.

"We?" said Chiun. "We lost nobody."

"He's dead. I don't know how they got to him but he's dead."

"Lots of people die," said Chiun, supremely confident of the eternal fact of mankind.

"Not like this, not when we have assured upstairs that we were going to protect him," said Remo. What puzzled him as much as the impossibility of anyone else getting into this room was the strange way the body had been torn apart, almost like a mischievous child playing a game with its food.

A machine could have done it but there was no machine in sight. And a machine would not have toyed with Dr. Ravits. Nothing big enough to do what had been done could have gotten into the room, certainly not past Chiun.

Remo went to the walls again and pressed and jiggled. He popped two reinforcing bolts which told him none of the panels moved.

"Little Father, I'm stumped," he said.

"We are not stumped. Sinanju has been glorious for thousands of years before this green little country of yours, and it will be glorious for thousands of years hereafter. There is a death here. We commiserate with those who have suffered from this accident but we commiserate also with those killed in floods, by lightning, and by famine. Of famine we know well, serving the village of Sinanju," said Chiun.

In times like these, Chiun always referred to the original reason for men from Sinanju becoming assassins. The little Korean village had been so poor, legend had it, that they had to throw newborn babies into the bay because they could not afford to feed them. This problem, as well as Remo could estimate, had not existed for the last three thousand years. However, so far as Chiun was concerned, it was still a constant, valid, never-ending worry.

"This wasn't any accident," Remo said. "We were supposed to protect this guy and someone or something got in here to him. They got through me."

"Watch your mouth. I never want to hear you say

that again. Sinanju has never lost a person. How can we lose him? How could we have? He is not an emperor. He was a scientist working on we know not what, and possibly that killed him.

But *we* did not lose anyone."

"He's dead. *We* were supposed to keep him alive."

"*You* were supposed to keep him alive and you won't even wear a kimono."

"I don't feel good in kimonos," said Remo, who could never get used to them because they flapped. "We have a problem."

"Yes," said Chiun, "and do you know what that problem is?"

"We lost someone."

"No," said Chiun gravely. "For even if the world should say we lost someone, in a century or two centuries, the world will forget. This is the way of the world."

The parchmentlike face nodded slowly. Remo was surprised. Never before had he heard Chiun admit that disgrace would pass. Always before, the most feared disaster was loss of face—usually because of something Remo had done or failed to do. But now, looking at the body, watching Remo test the walls as he had been taught to do, Chiun had admitted what he had never admitted before. There was something worse than disgrace because disgrace would pass in time.

"We cannot leave now," Chiun continued. "The real problem is that if we leave now, we leave whatever killed to be dealt with in the future. We fight now, not for Smith, for Smith will pass. America will pass. All nations that are, will be no more in a thousand years. Even treasure passes, for in one time one thing is valued and in another time, another is valued."

Remo watched a fly settle on the remains of Dr. Ravits. Another buzzed around the contented cat, but because the cat could control its skin movements and automatically flick it off, the fly could not land for long.

"Our problem," Chiun said, "is that there is something here or that has been here that can enter a sealed room and kill with great and malicious power and we do not know what it is. If we do not defeat it now, it will remain for other generations to face, and without the knowledge of what it is, they might be destroyed."

"Is there anything like this in the history of past Masters of Sinanju?" asked Remo.

Chiun shook his head. The wisps of beard trembled.

"No. There have been, of course, climbing walls many feet high, even walls slicked with grease to impede progress. There have been passages into rooms; there have been those who can cast their thoughts into others to make them kill themselves. These were the most dangerous but they are gone now and certainly this person did not have the ability to do this to himself. Look at the muscles, how they are shredded."

"Like somebody played with him," Remo said.

"But we have one advantage," said Chiun. And with his long fingernails, he made the signs of symbols which could not be translated and of course could not be overheard.

Remo read the long fingernails arcing and stabbing through the laboratory air.

"Let future generations know that the Master Chiun and his student Remo did face the first of the killers who knew no walls but took delight and played in death."

"Swell," Remo said. "We've got a problem and you're writing your autobiography."

Remo called Dara Worthington to let her know

there had been a little sort of an accident in Dr. Ravits' lab.

"What sort of accident?"

"See for yourself. And, Dara?"

"Yes."

"Bring a lot of paper towels. The real absorbent kind," Remo said.

When Dara Worthington saw what was left of Dr. Ravits, she turned purple and then white and then fell into Remo's arms. When she recovered Remo had her upright and was explaining that he had just discovered something wonderful. It would do even more of what Dr. Ravits had been working on than even Dr. Ravits could dream of.

Dara was not, at that time, particularly interested. She thought Remo should have a little more sensitivity toward the tragedy of a colleague than to be boasting about his prowess as a scientist.

Remo left Dara fuming at him, shaken by Dr. Ravits' death. He and Chiun went to all the other small rooms in the laboratory building. At each one, Remo let the occupants know that he was on the verge of a great discovery, one that would outdo everything that Dr. Ravits had tried to do.

"Bit confident, aren't you?" said one researcher.

"We have it locked already," Remo said with a smile and a wink.

And after telling everyone in the lab about his great new discovery, without even saying what it did, he and Chiun settled down, waiting to be attacked.

But they weren't. The only thing that happened was an incident with a strange dog coming out of an alley. It was strange because unlike other mad dogs, it did not charge as if in a pack with teeth bared, but rather used its own body weight to attack, as if it had the size and power of a rhino.

For an animal that size—no more than fifty pounds —Remo could take its charge and pass it on through, either letting the animal go, or, if it were truly dangerous, snapping the neck on the pass through. But this time, as his hand went out, he felt the animal push slightly behind his grasp and Remo had to reach for it and in so doing drove a finger into the neck. He had not intended to kill the poor mad dog.

Anyone watching would have seen nothing but a dog charge, miss and then land dead on the other side of the man it had charged. They would not even have seen Remo's hand move. But Chiun saw the finger go out after the animal.

"If you had worn a kimono, you would never have missed like that," he said.

"I don't know how I missed. It felt right. It was a dog. I know that."

"A kimono will make you almost adequate," Chiun said, folding his dark gold-and-green sunset kimono around his body. "I know that."

They announced where they were staying for the night and kept visible all night in windows so that whoever had killed Ravits would come after them,

But no one came.

The police had not been able to investigate the killing at the IHAEO labs because it was diplomatic territory and thus inviolate.

The IHAEO itself could not investigate the killing at the lab because that would require someone who knew how to investigate a killing or someone who knew how to investigate anything. What the IHAEO had was a young Dara Worthington, lusciously filling out a tight blouse, reporting to one of the thirty-two committees in the New York City offices of IHAEO.

This day, members actually attended the meeting

on "Security and the Inalienable Rights of Struggling Oppressed Peoples." This latter group included only those at war with America or one of her Western allies. Anyone fighting a Communist or Third World nation was not struggling or oppressed. Some observers from "liberation" groups were on the committee. They carried out their struggles with oppression from the finest restaurants, theaters and hotels in the world, paid for mainly by the American taxpayer.

They listened to Dara Worthington explain the death of an employee and thought about what she would look like without her blouse. There had once been an informal bidding war among IHAEO executives as to who would get her, until they realized that she was one of "those."

The man who had been killed in the lab in Washington was also one of "those."

"Those" were scientists who knew which end of the microscope to look through, secretaries who knew the alphabet and budget directors who actually knew what a budget was.

"Those" were the dull necessary drones one had to put up with and, even on some rare occasions like this, to listen to. The members of the committee on Security and Inalienable Rights knew the luscious Miss Worthington was a drone in a lovely body because she wanted to talk facts.

She talked of how the body was discovered, that there was no way anyone could have entered the lab because a new scientist happened to be standing at the lab door during the whole time. The new scientists couldn't be blamed because Dr. Ravits had been killed in such a bloody fashion that the murderer would have had to get himself covered with blood. There was no way either of the two men could have done the killing, no way anyone else could have entered, and yet Dr. Ravits was still dead.

Because of his work on the Ung beetle which was devastating the crops of central Africa and therefore threatening to starve millions, Dr. Ravits' death was a serious blow to millions of lives.

One of the African delegates suddenly snapped out of his doze.

"Did she say endives? Did she say there was trouble with the endives for the salad?" he whispered to the representative of the People's Liberation Organization of Lower Chad.

"No. Lives. Blow to lives, she said."

"Oh," said the other African delegate. "Then the endives are all right for the salad."

"Yes, of course."

"These meetings get so wearing that I just stop listening. When do we condemn America?"

"At the end, of course."

"You'll wake me up?"

"I'll vote for you," said the representative of the People's Liberation Organization of Lower Chad.

"Good chap. The salad for dinner is not in danger then. You're sure?"

"No. I told you."

"Thank you," said the observer delegate.

Dara Worthington outlined the problems with security, noted that the FBI had been withdrawn just before the murder but also noted that no other country had been able to defend the scientists either.

However, despite this tragedy, Dr. Ravits' work had been successful. The computer printout he had been reading at the time of his tragic death showed that finally the Ung beetle could be beaten and therefore millions of lives saved in Africa. There was a pheromone which Dr. Ravits had isolated, which could control the reproduction of the dreaded insect.

A hand shot up from the committee chairman.

"Is this going to go on much longer?" he asked.

"It's a major breakthrough in saving lives in central Africa," Dara said.

"That's good," said the chairman, who came from one of the central African countries. "We all care about saving lives in the Third World. But do you have to go into such extensive detail?"

"You mean about how the beetle can be eradicated?"

"Yes," the chairman said.

"The pheromone is ready to go," Dara said.

"Anything else?"

"You can start the procedures against the dreaded Ung beetle at any time now."

"Of course we will look into it," he said.

"I would suggest right away. The rainy season is beginning and if the Ung is allowed to reproduce—"

"Miss Worthy, we need no lectures about the rainy season from a white woman. We who are from Africa have lived too long with the patronizing attitude of the First World. We come from lands of the rainy season. We do not need to hear about rainy seasons from your sweet pulpy lips. I would suggest you examine your own virulent racism. I would be glad to instruct you in your shortcomings any evening you choose. Do I have a second on the motion?"

All hands shot up, even though there had been no motion.

The meeting was adjourned with a call to combat racism.

There were a few comments on how immature Miss Worthington was to be so crude about procedures. Some even mentioned that if she were in another branch of IHAEO, she might be dismissed on the spot.

But since she had to deal with the drones, as the
members of IHAEO liked to call those funny men in
white coats who did things with microscopes and
chemicals, she had to be tolerated.

They all had to be tolerated because the press-
relations people said that IHAEO had to have them.
Most of these delegates did not have to put up with
such problems in their home countries. There, when
you ran a government, you ran it. You didn't have to
go around pleasing people, and if the citizens didn't
like what was going on, they had better keep their
mouths shut.

But since ninety-nine percent of the funding for
IHAEO came from First World countries, mainly
America, one had to accommodate their unprogressive
ways. If they felt that a health organization actually
had to have people running around in white coats
doing things with microscopes and injecting bush
people with medicines, even though those people
never affected a Third World government in any way,
well, then the committee members of IHAEO would
put up with it. But only because their own press people
said so.

But they didn't have to have those sorts of people
around their plush-carpeted meeting rooms. They
certainly wouldn't want to dine with them in Paris and
London. None of those drones knew how to properly
condemn imperialism, racism or Zionism. They were
such backward boors that they did not understand the
sophisticated intricacies of staff meetings, interorgani-
zational conferences, grand international seminars.
They thought health had something to do with giving
babies injections, babies who weren't even the
children of important people. Just babies. Just because
they were going to die without medicine. These whites

—they were always white—would go around giving medicine to tribes that didn't even matter.

It was just like the old colonialism with white doctors treating Africans. And everyone on the committee found that objectionable. And so when the young white woman suggested that white doctors go running into African countries, acting like the old colonialists, treating anyone they wished, the Committee on Security and the Inalienable Rights of Struggling Oppressed Peoples not only voted to condemn the usual imperialism, racism and Zionism, but gave her a warning:

"Miss Worthington, we don't want to hear about rainy seasons in the bush again. Who do you think you are? If we were really in the bush, we would sell you for three goats and a jug of banana wine."

It came as a very great shock, therefore, when two hours later they were all informed that they were going to fly to central Africa to, of all things, fight bugs. The offices of Paris were informed. Cocktail parties were canceled. In rooms with fabulous carpets and furniture from Louis XIV, delegates listened in disbelief and sent telexes asking for confirmation of the message.

"Repeat message," they asked.

And it was repeated, "All IHAEO delegates to be ready for flight to Uwenda for pheromone treatment of Ung beetle menace."

"My Lord," gasped one coordinating executive director of IHAEO—there were forty-seven of them, all making more than a hundred thousand dollars a year because on less, no one could reasonably live in civilized life in a major city—"I came from Uwenda. I don't want to go back there ever. What sort of career move is that?"

In his palatial suite near the United Nations head-
quarters in New York, Amabasa François Ndo,
director general of IHAEO, heard the chorus of
complaints from delegates in all the major capitals of
Europe and the Americas. Did he realize that his
continued presence as director general of IHAEO
depended on those delegates? If they actually had to
leave Paris and Rome and New York and Beverly Hills
and Las Vegas to go to central Africa, he could expect
a revolt.

Was he ready to handle a massive delegate revolt?

Was he ready to be stripped of his rank?

Was he himself ready to be returned to the bush as
he so cavalierly had ordered all the delegates?

"Yes," answered Amabasa François Ndo.

Yes to all the questions.

Because he would do anything never to have to see
that kimono again.

6

Dara Worthington had left the meeting crying. After years of losing scientists while struggling against what had to be the most resilient insect on the face of the earth, the IHAEO labs and poor Dr. Ravits had finally succeeded in isolating a single chemical substance that could conquer the plague of central Africa.

And now, she had blundered somehow in the intricacies of IHAEO politics. Perhaps she had just lost touch with the organization's administration while she was working with the scientists. Whatever. But somehow she had ruined the one chance the people of central Africa had to survive the rainy season. She had taken the lifelong work of Dr. Ravits and at a simple committee meeting thrown it all away.

She had done everything wrong. She cried all the way back to Washington. There was an IHAEO jet leaving but the executive director of the coordinating committee of Liberation Front Observers needed all the available space for his cases of Dom Perignon, so Dara had to take a Greyhound bus.

Back at the laboratory, she did not know how she could face the researchers, all of whom knew that Dr. Ravits had finally solved the unsolvable problem of the invincible Ung beetle. Thousands, perhaps millions of people, might live because of his work and now it wasn't even going to be tried out.

She thought briefly of taking Ravits' solution to an American or French health unit. But if word got out that she was subverting the IHAEO by going to a First World country, no self-respecting Third World country would let in any medical teams at all. She learned quickly, when she had gone to work for IHAEO, that in dealing with a Third Worlder one was always dealing with that great unmentionable: "inferiority complex."

It clouded everything. It even defined Third World.

It was not a matter of being non-white because then Japan would be part of the Third World and it was not. In fact, nations that could be considered white were part of the Third World, whose membership requirement seemed to be that its populations were incapable of producing anything beneficial for the rest of mankind.

"Garbage countries," as one economist put it. "The only economic role they ever play is that they happen to breed over resources that industrial nations need. Then the industrial nations give them money which they spend back in the industrial nations because they don't produce anything worth buying themselves."

Dara Worthington could not agree with that cold assessment. People were not garbage even if their government showed no concern for their own populations. She had done missionary work with her parents in Africa and found the people kind and lovely. She loved the people and therefore would put up with anything to help them. She had seen those poor countries suffer the ravages of insect plagues. She had seen proud, decent African farmers facing fields, which they and their families had poured years of work into, that had turned into useless shreds of crops because insects had gotten to them first.

In more advanced countries, a disaster like that would mean that the farmers would lose money and, at worst, have to go on to another job. But in the Third World it meant what it had meant for thousands of years since man had come out of the caves. It meant death.

That was why Dara Worthington had gone to work for the IHAEO. That was why she could easily put up with the machinations and humiliations of being part of the scientific element of the IHAEO. She didn't care if hundreds of millions were spent on private planes, and if fortunes were spent on luxurious mansions. At least some money was going to help people who needed help and that was important to her. That was her department's responsibility and because she had lost her head and said outright to a committee of the IHAEO that they would have to do something now, before the rainy season, she had failed. If she had not been so desperate, so upset by Dr. Ravits' death, she never would have confronted them like that. Instead, she would have found a willing delegate, bought him an expensive dinner, and gotten him to make the proposal. He would then, of course, take all the credit for the work and present it as a Third World achievement. It didn't matter to her; it was the way things worked.

But this time she had failed and she cried all the way back to Washington. At the laboratory complex, she found the new scientists, apparently undisturbed by the death of their colleague. The elderly Oriental asked why she was crying. The sexy, obnoxious American seemed more intent on boasting about an even greater discovery that would eclipse that of poor Dr. Ravits.

"I am crying because I think that by my foolishness I have condemned thousands of people to death."

"Since when are you a graduate of West Point or Annapolis?" asked Remo.

"You're a beast," said Dara.

"One learns to tolerate him," Chiun said.

"How do you?" said Dara.

"I must say that sometimes I do not know," Chiun said.

"I'm still not wearing a kimono," Remo said.

"He refuses to wear a kimono?" Dara asked Chiun.

Chiun nodded wisely.

"How sad," she said.

"You are wise beyond your years," Chiun said.

"No. If I were truly wise I would have gotten Dr. Ravits' discovery accepted by the IHAEO."

"Why is that a problem?" Remo asked.

"You wouldn't understand," Dara said.

"Maybe I would," said Remo. "Then again, maybe I wouldn't."

Dara explained about the Third World politics within the IHAEO.

"You're right," said Remo. "I wouldn't understand, but look. We'd all like to see this experiment work. I think it would probably attract an awful lot of people."

"Not the killers?" said Dara. "We've had enough killing here."

"Maybe not enough," said Remo, thinking of the killers who were still alive.

"How can you say anything so cruel?"

"I move my lips," Remo said.

"We wish to help," said Chiun.

"You're so kind."

"One learns kindness when one lives every day with ingratitude," Chiun said.

"But you can't help. You don't understand the intricacies of the Third World and Third World politics, especially on the international level."

"Who do we have to reach?" Remo asked.

"You can't reach them. They're an international body. They have diplomatic immunity. They're all wealthy from their jobs. They can't be bought. Nothing can be done."

"Who is the most powerful man in the IHAEO?" Remo asked.

"Amabasa Francois Ndo. He is the director general."

"Where is he?"

"He is supposed to fly in this afternoon from Paris," Dara said.

"What tribe is he?" asked Chiun.

"You wouldn't refer to the director general as a member of a tribe," she said.

"But what tribe?" Chiun insisted.

"I really don't know."

"We will find out," said Chiun.

"You must never refer to the director general as a member of a tribe," said Dara. "You'll never get anywhere like that. He would have his bodyguards throw you right out of the room, maybe out the window. He is a very proud man."

"You just get Dr. Ravits' discoveries ready for us and we'll take care of convincing Ndo," Remo said.

"You mean the anti-immune pheromone molecules," she said.

"Right. That," said Remo.

"Absolutely that," said Chiun. After all, they were supposed to be scientists.

Amabasa François Ndo heard his pilot announce in his clipped British accent that the IHAEO diplomatic jet was about to land at Kennedy International Airport. He burned a little sliver of châteaubriand before the god Ga, a wooden replica made from the first willow to bend in the first storm of the rain season. A good Ga protected one during dangerous times. A good Ga could take an Inuti boy and make him a great man, make him a director general of a worldwide organization.

Ndo always had the Ga with him. He had brought it with him to the Sorbonne, when he was young and poor, living on the pittance paid by the French colonial government.

They had sent him to school where he became part of the revolutionary movement to remove France from Inuti lands. The French had built roads for the Inuti, established police for the Inuti, hospitals for the Inuti, laws for the Inuti lands. But the French lived in the big houses and the Inuti served them drinks on cool white porches as their untouchable cool white ladies looked on.

Amabasa François Ndo had two ambitions as a young man going to Paris for his education. One was to become the head of police, the other was to have one of those cool white women.

The second ambition was realized seven minutes after he rented a cheap room. He didn't even have time to unpack. The daughter of an industrialist, determined to end racism in the world, came into his room calling for a form of solidarity against people whom Ndo figured out were just like her father.

She issued this call while undressing him and herself. It was her favorite way of fighting racism. Unfortunately, Ndo, like all the other African students she met, needed penicillin to escape the ravages of solidarity with the young woman.

Amabasa hoped his other ambition proved more satisfying. But he abandoned it when he saw how police-men lived compared to how ambassadors lived. He had a knack for seeing where movements went and gliding along with them. He also found he had a knack for eating at fine restaurants, and more than a knack for public speaking.

When an African student raped and then hacked to death a local Parisian girl, he knew immediately it was a case of a madman who should be put away but he also knew that all Africans would be blamed by some whites and that might eventually affect him.

So he took his last piece of a stolen crepe and burned it before Ga secretly in his Paris room. The smoke rose and he chanted requests for protection. Then he went out and made the first of his speeches about the ravages of French colonialism as if the only reason anyone could commit such a mad brutal murder was a century of oppression. He put on trial all the things and people he so envied: the gendarmes, the law courts, the big white houses and even the cool white women.

Surprisingly, none of the young white radical women were offended. They wanted to hear whites attacked, their fathers attacked, their brothers attacked, their lovers attacked.

This realization stood the young Inuti student well, because in an instant he understood that there was nothing so fraudulent or so malicious that would not attract support from some white groups, provided they agreed with the choice of target.

With proper respect for Ga, a brilliant appreciation of abstract concepts and a disregard for truth that would have gotten him stoned out of any Inuti village, Amabasa François Ndo rose in the ranks of Third World diplomacy.

It did not matter that First World nations supported

the IHAEO. The way to success was not gratitude but treating white nations like those white radical girls so long ago in Paris. Applause followed. Awards. Honors from the white countries he attacked. Occasionally there were efforts to turn the health organization into some form of international clinic but Ndo always managed to convince members to address broader issues. Colonialism was a health issue. Imperialism was a health issue. And when Russia weighed in, totally on the side of the Arabs, Zionism became a health issue.

Considering the makeup of the delegates, these were easier issues to deal with. Ndo was sure there weren't three delegates who knew a corpuscle from a tractor trailer. Most of them did have college degrees but had gotten them in sociology which made them virtually useless for anything but unfounded speeches anyway. He would never express that opinion, of course, because of the strong support of most sociologists for IHAEO. Not that he would ever let his son become one.

Amabasa François Ndo was at the pinnacle of his career when his private jet landed at Kennedy International Airport and his bodyguards motioned his armor-plated Cadillac limousine in from the hangar. He took the small wooden god and put it into the vest pocket of his three-piece Saville Row suit and prepared to debark. There had been some recent troubles with America threatening to withdraw its funding unless IHAEO started doing more health and less politicizing, but that would be easily quelled by a stroke of good fortune.

The stroke of good fortune was Dr. Ravits. One of the drones had been killed in the laboratory which had been having nothing but trouble since it started. They were always having killings there, and to Ndo the lab was nothing but a pain. None of the employees seemed politically aware and they certainly didn't know how to throw a party and if they weren't necessary for public relations in the West, he wouldn't have had them at all. But now this Ravits person had gotten himself killed and Ndo was going to use it.

That was why he was flying into New York City: to address the United Nations on one more attempt to destroy IHAEO.

Ndo loved New York, loved the skyline, loved it even more than Paris. New York was power and action and all those wonderful furriers from which he supplied his girlfriends and his sons' girlfriends.

He didn't like the people, of course, but then again, he never had to meet any of them. They rode in subways and they walked on the streets. Ndo never did either.

He got clearance from his bodyguards to descend and walked down the stairway from the jetcraft to his limousine and found two men waiting for him in the backseat.

One wore a kimono. The other wore a black T-shirt and black slacks.

"Who gave you permission to ride in the car with me?" asked Ndo.

"Hi," said Remo pleasantly. "We've come on business."

"I do not discuss business except by appointment."

"Your secretary was uncooperative too," Remo said. "He is in the front seat."

Ndo glanced into the front seat. A very big man was curled up in a fetal position. The big man was his favorite bodyguard and could break someone's arm with one hand. Ndo had seen him do it. His favorite bodyguard was not moving.

"Ah, business, yes," said the director general of IHAEO. "Well, I am on my way to the United Nations. Let us do our business quickly."

Ndo gave the pair his most attentive look, even while he set off his emergency alarm to alert body-guards and local police. Ndo had long-standing orders on what to do if he was abducted. The long-standing orders were to give any terrorists exactly what they wanted if they would return Ndo unharmed. Of course, he had already eliminated the danger from most of the terrorists in the world by putting them on the IHAEO payroll.

Ndo listened politely to some claptrap about bugs and laboratory experiments and a rainy season. He listened until he saw the blue bubble of a police car in front and then another one in back. Gas suddenly filled the backseat but he knew enough to hold his breath. A dark mask fell down from the car's ceiling. He pulled it over his face and breathed pure oxygen.

He waited for a full count of four hundred, far longer than anyone could hold his breath. Then he pressed the gas-exhaust lever and waited until there was absolutely no trace left in the backseat, then replaced the mask in its compartment. The police would have to take care of the bodies.

But there were no bodies. The white man just continued talking. He was still talking about bugs when Ndo tried to stab him with a little ceremonial knife he carried. The knife had the poison of the Gwee bush. It would send anyone cut with it into painful paralysis, like an execution which took a week of dying, every moment in agony.

The knife somehow wouldn't cut the man's skin. Remo put it away on the floor.

"So that's what we want," he said finally. "The good points are that you are going to help millions.

The bad points are that if you don't do it, we are going to take off your face."

"I am not afraid," Ndo said.

Remo pressured the thumb up against the forearm, creating a shock through Ndo's nervous system. But he accepted the pain, accepted it as he had learned to accept pain for the initiation ceremony of the Inuti.

Remo cracked the thumb and still the man didn't surrender. He did not surrender as his ribs strained close to his heart, even though sweat began to pour from his forehead. Then, with a smile, Ndo passed out.

"I don't want to kill him, Little Father," Remo said. "We need him to give orders."

"He is afraid of death," Chiun said. "But not of pain."

"I've never seen anything like that," Remo said.

"Because you have not adequately studied the history of the Masters of Sinanju."

"I have," Remo said.

"Not adequately."

Remo glanced at the police cars. Uniformed officers stood alongside the cars, guns down. He did not want to have to hurt them.

"Not adequately," Chiun repeated.

"I don't care," Remo said. "I'm not wearing a kimono."

"If you had read the histories, you would," Chiun said.

"What do the histories say about kimonos that's of any help?"

"The histories say that only pale pieces of pigs' ears refuse to wear the kimono."

"Where does it say that?" Remo asked. "I'm the first white Master ever."

"It says it in the latest history of Sinanju, called 'The

Persecution of Chiun' or 'How Benevolence Is Never Rewarded.' "

"Skip that. What about this guy?" Remo said.

"The Inuti are like that. They once had great emperors. It is manhood training he used to resist your pain. Don't worry. The Inuti are a reasonable people," Chiun said.

"Meaning that they paid their assassins," Remo said.

"In goats and goat products. But at least on time," Chiun said. He reached into the vest pocket of the diplomat's three-piece suit. With a gentle working of the nerve endings around his solar plexus, Chiun brought the director general of IHAEO back to consciousness.

"You are Inuti," said Chiun, who had told Remo before that to know the tribe of an African was to know the man. Unlike whites, Chiun had said, Africans had a history and loyalty to their villages. No proper African would defy his father as Remo defied Chiun.

Ndo smiled. It was a cold smile because pain was still in his body but it was a smile of triumph.

"We are Sinanju," said Chiun.

Ndo had heard the tales of the dreaded ones from the Orient who had served the ancient kings of the Inuti.

"What does Sinanju care about bugs?" asked Ndo.

"Sinanju cares about what Sinanju cares about," said Chiun.

"Whereas I respect the House of Sinanju, my hands are not my own," Ndo said. "I have obligations, commitments. What can I do for you other than this?"

"When Sinanju wants something else, it will ask for something else," Chiun said. "Tell me, Inuti, do you think that your ancient conquest of pain is enough to build the wall that stops Sinanju?"

And with that he held before Ndo his Ga, the little wooden statue. Ndo was fast but his hands were like great slow muffins compared to the speed of the long fingernails. Ndo reached but the statue was out of his grasp.

Slowly Chiun broke off Ga's right leg. Ndo wept.

"Ga's manhood is next," Chiun said.

"No," cried Ndo. "Do not. My seed will die with it."

"So, Inuti, we understand each other," said Chiun.

Ndo offered to make Chiun the wealthy director of any agency he wished but Chiun's answer again was:

"Sinanju cares about what Sinanju cares about."

"You mean we all have to go into the bush to look at bugs? There will be a revolt."

"There will be the glorious vindication of Dr. Ravits' work," Chiun said.

"Dr. who?"

"One of the scientists," said Chiun.

"I don't know them. Who heads his department?"

"Dara Worthington," Remo said.

"I don't know her. Who is her director?"

Both Remo and Chiun shrugged.

"Give me Ga and I will find out," Ndo said.

"You will find out because I have Ga and will keep him until you do," Chiun said.

Ndo looked at the old Oriental, then dropped his eyes and nodded.

As he waved the police away and told them it was all a misunderstanding, he heard the two men from Sinanju talking. They were arguing about kimonos and Ndo knew he never wanted to see a kimono again in his life.

7

Waldron Perriweather III watched the news on television, heard the commentators talk about the good work of IHAEO and its fight to prevent famine; heard what was billed as the final battle against the evil Ung beetle.

He stormed into the laboratory on his estate and promptly passed out from the DDT. When he recovered he asked just how much DDT his entomologist was using now and when he was told, he commented that surely everything must be ready by now.

"Not yet, Mr. Perriweather, but soon," the scientist said.

'Just let me know when everything will be ready," said Perriweather.

He had his lawyers find out certain things about the demonstration IHAEO was going to mount to show the world how it was fighting against famine.

When he learned the demonstration would be outside, in the fields of central Africa, he muttered a small "damn" under his breath. "Still," he mumbled, "sometimes it can work outside. We'll see."

Nathan and Gloria Muswasser did not want to see millions of man's fellow creatures poisoned painfully to death. They could not bear to wait around for another injustice before the inalienable rights of all creatures were protected under the law.

They would strike now. They loaded the barrels of TNT onto the rented truck and drove it to the front gate of the IHAEO laboratories in Washington, D.C.

"Order by two of your new members. Part of their great new breaththrough," Nathan called out to the guard. They delivered the TNT to the crates being loaded for the Ung-beetle demonstration in central Africa.

They did not stay to see the barrels loaded but turned the truck around quickly and drove away. They drove for twenty minutes and then Gloria said to Nathan:

"Do you make the phone call or do I?"

"I don't know. This is my first time. I feel so relevant," said Nathan Muswasser.

"The hottest place in hell," said Gloria Muswasser, "is reserved for those who in a time of crisis do nothing. Or something like that."

"I'll make the call. You're too nervous," said Nathan. He went into a telephone booth near a diner and dialed a local television station.

The paper he held trembled in his hands. Finally he was doing something for the world.

As soon as he heard the newsman's voice, he read the statement on the paper:

"We, the Species Liberation Alliance, take full and total credit for the revolutionary act this day at the murderous center of oppression, the IHAEO laboratories in Washington, D.C. We, the core cadres of the SLA, call upon all people to join us in our just and legitimate struggle against the oppressors of all creatures. Other liberating acts will follow."

"What are you talking about?" the newsman asked.

"I am talking, man, about the explosion at the IHAEO labs. We must have killed at least two hundred people, man." Nathan Muswasser liked calling people "man"; it made him feel relevant.

"No explosion at the labs, buddy," the newsman said.

"You're lying. We did it. We're claiming credit. It's our revolutionary act and we have a right to get credit."

"There wasn't any explosion," the reporter insisted.

"Listen, man," Nathan said. "We bought the dynamite. We planted the dynamite. We set the fuse and we want credit. It's our act."

"Can't give you credit; you haven't killed anyone," the reporter answered.

"What's going on here? Let me talk to the station manager," Nathan said.

Gloria, seeing Nathan turn red and hearing his voice rise, leaned out of the cab of the truck and yelled, "What's the matter?"

Nathan covered the speaker with his hand.

"They won't give us credit, honey."

"What?" screamed Gloria.

"The guys says we can't get credit."

"Dammit," snarled Gloria. "Let me speak to him." She climbed out of the cab of the truck. Nathan handed her the telephone.

"I told him we planted the dynamite."

"TNT, dummy," she snapped. Into the telephone, she said, "Okay, what's the matter?"

"Nothing's the matter," the reporter said. "This station is not giving credit without deaths. If you want credit without deaths, try some wire service. We are just not giving credit for bombings or any kind of killing anymore without some real killing going on. New policy."

"We had to have five hundred pounds of TNT," she said. "Do you know how much that is? We had the best fuse and I checked it myself. If my husband had checked it, I might say all right, but I checked it, and I get things right. Now that thing went off at the height of the work hours. We set it for when there'd be the maxium number of people there."

"Lady, it's not up to me," the reporter said. "Just two months ago we got a call from a liberation group that wanted credit for blowing up a day school. They say they killed 350 kids. We sent a reporter out and you know what he found?"

Gloria didn't answer; she was still fuming.

"Do you know what he found?"

"What?"

"There were no 350 dead preschoolers. There wasn't even a nosebleed. The flowers were growing in the schoolyard. The sun was shining and the mothers were picking up their children. Now where would we be if we went ahead and gave credit for that?"

"Who was it?" Gloria asked. "Which liberation group? Maybe I know them."

"I don't know. One of them. It was valid. It had a lot of support. Church groups. Professors."

"Oh, that kind," Gloria said in dismissal. "Anybody can get professors. But that's not us. We're the SLA. We have a tradition. You know we're good for those deaths. We've been good before," said Gloria. "What about the pilot? Those farmers? The oil drillers? That entomologist? They're all ours, you know. The people who did those are dead but the struggle continues."

"I'm sorry. We just can't give credit anymore without the bodies."

"What's he saying?" Nathan asked.

"Shh," said Gloria. "Look, we planted the damn thing. I'm sure it went off."

"Sorry. Station policy," the newsman said.

"You know, it's people like you who make this a crud world," Gloria said as she slammed down the telephone.

"No credit?" asked Nathan.

"Not for even a bruise."

"What went wrong?"

"Nothing went wrong," Gloria said. "Just a bunch of fascists at that damned station. Little men running big things."

"Maybe we should have heard the explosion," Nathan said. "Even this far away."

"I don't know. Come on. Let's get out of here. Sometimes these stations sicken me, you know?"

"Yeah," said Nathan. "What the hell. We still have the thing that'll do the real damage."

"You didn't forget that, did you?" Gloria asked.

"Are you kidding?"

"Maybe it won't work out-of-doors, did you ever think of that?" Gloria said.

"No," said Nathan.

"Then again, it might work better outdoors," she said. "We might get some real good numbers without walls to prevent it from spreading."

"We'll get credit then," Nathan said.

"Who knows? You go out of your way. You buy the best materials, you buy the best fuses, you triple-check them and nothing. Not even a bruise."

"You don't think it went off then?" Nathan asked.

"No, it didn't go off," snarled Gloria. Sometimes Nathan was enough to send her up a wall.

"Should we go back and check?"

"No, dummy. They would probably have people waiting for us."

At the lab, Dara Worthington threw the defective

detonator in a separate trashcan and had the barrels of TNT carefully carted away from the area by police. The would-be terrorists forgetting to erase the TNT markings from the sides of the barrels and being spotted by a cautious workman, had been her second lucky break.

But the biggest break of the day had been the announcement by Director General Ndo that IHAEO was going to mount a major effort, immediately, against the Ung beetle. They were calling the world in to watch. Everyone was going to be there. Even the IHAEO delegates.

She didn't know what had produced the turnabout in the IHAEO position. All she had done was mention to that nice old Oriental gentleman in the kimono the troubles she had, and a few hours later, Ndo made his announcement.

Well, she wasn't one to look gift horses in the mouth. She would take her good luck where she found it. Maybe now, she thought, IHAEO would see what could be done and they might devote more funds to fighting disease and pestilence. There was hope now. And she wasn't going to let this afternoon's crude attempt at mass murder discourage her.

With the TNT out of the way, she made one last inspection of the laboratory. Oddly enough, Dr. Ravits' cat had gone crazy. It had thrown itself against the reinforced steel plate walls of the laboratory and somehow smashed itself to death. There were three small lines cut sharp into the steel just above the small cat's body.

If Dara didn't know better, she would have sworn that the three lines were claw marks.

But she did know better. No cat's claws were ever able to score steel.

8

Harold W. Smith finally made contact with Remo. He was taking Barry Schweid out for some sun when one latch clip on the case popped open. That was the sign. There was no beep, no buzzer, nothing to attract attention. Smith had designed it that way because he did not want people alerted to the fact that he was being contacted.

Smith opened the case on the small keyboard that looked like an ultraportable computer, he punched in the proper code for receiving a call. Then he put the microthin line to his ear.

Schweid saw all this but only cared about how the storage access related to the communications modem. He had to be reminded by Smith not to disconnect him. So while Barry played with the workings inside the case, Smith talked. They continued to walk down the rutted dirt road to a boat which would take Barry snorkeling at one of the safest beaches on the island.

"Smitty, we had a bit of a problem at the lab," came Remo's voice.

"I know. They buried the sponge with Dr. Ravits' remains today. I made a promise to someone else because you made a promise to me."

"I don't know how it happened," Remo said. "We

blew it. But we think we're going to nail these guys now."

"I hope so. This is a greater danger than people realize," Smith said, thinking of the Ung beetle's ability to counteract all known poisons and how dangerous it would be if that ability spread to other creatures. It was as if there was a giant chess game going on over what species would survive. Why anyone would champion the cause of insects over people, Smith did not know, but he did know that this new world somehow seemed to tolerate the most outrageous of acts. It seemed that the more mindless and more virulent the group, the greater support it got from the placard wavers and the marchers.

It sometimes seemed to him that the fabric of civilization itself had been torn and the last threads were being shredded. But because of the way he had been raised, he would defend those last threads because that was all there was.

"Remo," he said, "that experiment against the beetle in central Africa has got to work."

"I'll be there," Remo said.

"You were at the lab," Smith said.

"But this time I think they've got to be coming at me and Chiun," Remo said.

"Good luck then."

"Smitty, you worry too much."

"Don't you worry?"

"Sure, sometimes. But then I forget what I was worrying about," Remo said.

"Good luck anyway," Smith said.

Barry Schweid was working the keys as Smith spoke. Smith had gotten the young computer genius into light summer pants and a short-sleeved shirt, gotten a waterproof container for his piece of blue blanket. Barry was even getting a tan and eating vegetables.

Smith could never quite tan. He would redden in
degrees and if he got enough sun he would burn. St.
Martin seemed to have the hottest sun in the Caribbean and he was using a total sunblock to protect his
skin. He wore checkered shorts and a plaid sports
shirt, but even strolling along the dusty roads toward
the eastern side of the island among passing herds of
cows and wandering goats, he looked as if he were
attending a conference down some hall. He just
couldn't get away from it.

"They'd better do well," Barry said.

"Who?" said Smith.

"I don't know who," said Barry. "But if they don't
do well, I wouldn't give you much chance to save mankind."

Smith checked his earpiece to see if Barry could tap
in. He couldn't. He knew also that he had been talking
softly and Barry's hearing was almost nonexistent.
This was not because of any natural defect; it was
simply that Barry ignored all surroundings but his
computer.

And he was now looking at the organization's access
mode, inside Smith's briefcase, and shaking his head.

"What are you talking about, Barry?"

Barry explained in terms of numbers and masses of
numbers. He talked calculus and theoretical math and
Smith, despite a handful of technical college degrees,
could not follow him.

But by the time they reached the small enclosed bay
and the boat that would take them to a small flat
island a quarter-mile away, called Pinel, Smith had
gotten the gist of what Barry was saying.

While Smith had been talking to Remo, Barry had
been pulling from the computer's memories background data to test voice activation. The computer
had told him of two groups of competing organisms,

one large, the other small. So far, the large were in charge, but the access board warned Barry that this might soon change. Smith thought of men and insects.

Barry said, "The computer said that if the larger units don't stop the smaller units in this try, zowee. You see, this was all activated by whatever it was you were talking about on the phone. Anyway, it's going to be like Zorkmonster. Because the smaller units are headed toward a big final victory. This is a crucial one. Just like Zorkmonster."

"What's Zorkmonster?" Smith asked.

"It's a game. You play it with a joystick. It's called humans against the Zorkmonster, only when the Zorkmonster becomes invincible, he sets up a final battle at one point to try to trap you and wipe you out. You, of course, represent the humans."

"Of course," Smith said.

"At that time, there's only one way to beat Zorkmonster," Barry said.

"What is it?" Smith said quickly. He might try to reach Remo with this information.

"All you can do is unplug the machine. Zorkmonster never loses," Barry said.

The news media were generally ecstatic. Despite financial cutbacks from America, despite criticism from reactionary groups, the IHAEO now was making headway against the dreaded curse of central Africa, the Ung beetle.

Twenty-four jetloads of delegates arrived at the main airport of Uwenda, the country that now comprised five tribes including the Inuti.

Amabasa François Ndo was returning home in triumph.

A television announcer said: "We are witnessing here Africans helping Africans, despite Western white obstruction. We see here a triumph of indigenous peoples over their oppressors." The television announcer was from an American network.

The delegates' jets were met by air-conditioned limousines that stretched out along the roads, a caravan of wealth. Ndo, normally the darling of the press, refused all interviews. He had not slept well since Chiun had taken the god Ga from him. He recognized the hills outside the car and realized he was returning to his own home village. The horror hit him then that the village elders would demand he show them that he had safely kept Ga with him. But he did not have it for them.

Fortunately, he was on good terms with the president, vice-president, chief magistrate, chief of police, and head of the Agricultural Department of Uwenda. They were all his cousins. The commander in chief of the Army was his brother. Together, they might all keep the rest of the village at bay. Certainly he had shipped home enough money for them and they might just realize that if he stopped, the money stopped. Still, Ga was a powerful god. He was thinking these things as someone up front was talking white nonsense about the damned beetle they were all going to see get killed. They should have sent a fly swatter.

Yet the man in the kimono had insisted, so here he was, the director general of the IHAEO, in a stinking muddy village with people who didn't even know how to dress. Home, unsweet home.

An especially backward and despicable looking pair were fawning over the polish on his new limousine.

"Get those two out of there. They smell," Ndo said to his chauffeur.

"They say they're your parents, your Excellency."

"Oh well, put them in some clothes and get the photographer."

"Yes, your Excellency."

"And bathe them. Yes, god, bathe them."

"Yes, your Excellency."

The place was even worse than he imagined. The fields of maize were even more scraggly, the village square in the center of the huts dustier, and the roads were absolutely impassable. Come rainy season, they would be a sea of mud.

"The roads are awful. What happened to them?"

"The French left, your Excellency."

"They didn't take the roads with them, did they? Did they steal them?"

"They stopped repairing them, Excellency."

"All right, all right. Let's get this experiment over with and get back to where it's livable."

"The scientists have not arrived yet, your Excellency."

"Why not? What's holding them up?" asked Ndo, looking over the long line of dark roofs, the immaculate limousines stretched out like an expensive technological necklace through the yellow dried fields.

"There were only so many limousines to go around, Excellency," his aide said.

"So?"

"So the scientists are coming by ox cart."

Dara Worthington did not mind the ox cart. She did not mind the dust. She had been raised in country like this and it was good to get back to Africa, good to see the people again. Even good to ride in an ox cart again.

Remo and Chiun rode beside her with the other

scientists in the carts behind. At several points along the road, they had to pay road tolls.

What they were paying for was occasional patches of asphalt, left from the days of the French. Who they were paying were soldiers of the Uwenda Army.

The Uwenda Army performed other public functions. They collected money at the markets from both shoppers and vendors. They collected money from dice games. They collected cold cash from anyone who wanted to build anything in Uwenda.

Up ahead on the somewhat asphalt road, soldiers now were menacingly turning their machine guns toward the carts. Behind them was a tank, its large cannon also pointed at the small carts.

Dara had heard about a diplomatic tiff when the Soviets had given Uwenda seven tanks. The President for Eternity, Claude Ndo, had read in a British publication that the tanks Uwenda had received were not the most modern in the Soviet arsenal. He did not want second-line tanks.

A Soviet general was sent to Uwenda to explain to the President for Eternity, Claude Ndo, cousin of the director general of IHAEO, that the only difference between the first-line Soviet tank and the second line was a refractionary voltage regulator for use in arctic conditions.

"You have no need of the newer model," the general said.

"Do you need it?"

"We maneuver in arctic conditions," the Russian said.

"We have interests in freezing areas just like any other nation."

"Who are you going to fight in the arctic?" the general asked.

"Whoever we wish. Just like you."

"How are you going to get the tanks there?"

"Give us the tools and we will do the rest. We are your allies. The Third World stands in solidarity with you."

The general mumbled something about the need for the new tanks being ridiculous and was told that the Russians always had a reputation for being crude and insensitive. He was told that this crudeness might cost them allies in Africa. He was told that even now there was a movement in America to get more African allies.

The President for Eternity did not hear the Russian general mumble an old childhood prayer asking that all this might come to pass. The general faced a real problem: if Uwenda got the new tank, then every other African country would want the new tank.

Gabon, for instance, was not going to sit around while Tanzania had the new tank because that would mean a loss of face. And if Tanzania got the new tank, then of course, Mozambique, Zimbabwe and Ghana would also have to have the new tank.

It was a nightmare to contemplate so the Soviet general, as he had been instructed by the Soviet foreign office, pulled out a manila envelope.

"These are the plans to show you how your tank is as good as any around," the general said.

The President for Eternity opened the envelope and mumbled, "Not quite a large enough demonstration."

"Would you take a check for the rest?" said the general.

"I think that is good strategy," said the President for Eternity, taking the American hundred-dollar bills from the manila envelope. He insisted upon American dollars because Russians rubles always had to be converted into dollars anyway before they would buy anything worthwhile.

There was one more problem with the tanks that

now lined the roadways of Uwenda, looking like
magnets for dust.

"Where are the drivers? The people to use the radar
for the guns? The mechanics to fix the tanks? You are
not dealing with some fool. These things do not run
themselves," said Claude Ndo.

And so the general promised advisers also. What
Uwenda supplied was the Army officer to sit in the
cockpit and stiffly salute the President for Eternity
during parades.

One rainy season, the Russian mechanics became ill
and the entire armored corps of Uwenda stayed where
it was. By the time the Russians recovered, the tanks
had been cannibalized and only one could be made to
run again. This one now stood alongside the road,
protecting the ox-cart caravan which was bringing the
scientists who would try to fight the Ung beetle.

A soldier hopped from the top of the tank and
strolled up to the first cart. Dara put her body between
the soldier and the white refrigerated box holding the
chemical pheromones developed by Dr. Ravits.

Four other soldiers followed him. They all looked at
Dara Worthington and began lowering their pants.
Remo asked them once to pull up their pants. He asked
them twice. He even suggested a third time that they
do this.

Perhaps, Remo thought, they did not understand
English. This had been a French colony.

Remo spoke no French so he settled on a more
universal language. He yanked the AK-47 rifle from
the nearest soldier's hands and stuck it down the
soldier's pants and pulled the trigger. The soldier
jumped as if stung by bees, flipping backward, but
even as he did, Remo made sure he felt no pain. He
crushed the soldier's temple with a flick of a finger.

The other four soldiers understood the message

perfectly. Up came the pants. But so did their guns. Remo faded slowly to the left to draw their fire and Chiun faded slowly right. Guns barked in the hot central African dust like coughing machines. The bullets hit rocks, kicked up little beige showers of dust, shredded dry leaves, but missed the two of them.

The soldiers sprayed their shots and launched grenades and still the two looked like mirages floating out there, teasing the men with the guns.

The soldiers were not bad shots but unfortunately they were shooting only at what they saw. None of them had noticed that before the firing, the two men had begun to sway, ever so slightly, but rhythmically, like a snake charmer with a cobra, moving so that the movements locked eyes on them, then relaxed the eyes on them. Some of the soldiers actually hit what they thought they saw, but what they were looking for was never in front of their bullets.

Dara watched in astonishment as four soldiers emptied their guns around her, but always away from her. When the final pop was gone, she saw the two new scientists step out from behind the ox cart and casually remove the weapons from the soldiers and stack them up. Then they attached the soldiers to the carts with wires and used them to help the oxen move faster.

Cheers, soft at first, then louder, came from behind nearby rocks. Old women and children crept out. Then young women. Then men, some in just loincloths, some in tattered long pants.

They rushed up to the last remaining tank in the Uwenda armored arsenal. One jumped inside and started to pass out bundles. It was their food which the soldiers had stolen. Some of them recovered old trinkets they had treasured.

"*Vive la France!*" one cried, thinking all whites

were French. One of them asked in French when the French were coming back.

Chiun, who understood the old French, answered that they were not coming back. There were moans of sadness.

To Dara and Remo as the carts pulled closer to the Inuti village up ahead, Chiun explained that this had once been a thriving land of great Inuti kings, but then the white man had come and taught another way of life. It looked like a better way and for a while it was, but it required white men to run it.

The old ways of the Inuti were forgotten; the old kings discredited. The loyalty of king to subject and subject to king was ignored. The efficient Inuti way of farming was abandoned. Then the whites left.

And the poor tribesmen had neither white way nor traditional Inuti way to run anything.

"So once again, we see how white ways are wrong," Chiun said.

"I've never heard that explained so well, so beautifully," said Dara.

"I'm still not wearing a kimono," said Remo.

The carts arrived at a field that seemed to be undulating silver waves, glistening in the sun.

"The Ung beetle," said Dara. "It used to be kept under control naturally but since we've been fighting it, it's actually increased."

Then she turned in the cart and patted the white refrigerator box.

"This is going to change it all. It used to be such a beautiful land. This is going to give the land back to the people."

A runner emerged from the long line of black limousines, all with windows closed. The motors were running, the air conditioners on full blast.

"His excellency wants to know when you are ready to begin."

"In fifteen minutes," said Dara.

"He wants the machinery set up by the cars."

"It will work better in the middle of the field," she said.

"All right then. Signal when you are ready."

Dara ordered the carts into the middle of the field. The oxen twitched and almost bolted because the Ung beetles were all over them. Remo and Chiun released the Uwenda soldiers from the wires and they ran away, brushing the shiny bugs off them.

Dara stayed at the head of the cart. The other scientists rode too, some batting the bugs away, others trying just to ignore them.

"What are you two using? Give the rest of us some of it," Dara said.

"Using?" said Remo.

"That repellent. Why aren't the bugs landing on you?"

"Just keep your skin moving," Remo said.

"You mean you can control your own skin?"

"You mean you can't?" Remo said, remembering now the times before his training when mosquitoes used to bother him.

The carts reached the center of the field and the oxen were released to dash clumsily over the dry dead earth, away from the beetles which were devouring the last flimsy crop of the village.

Dara and the scientists prepared small canisters from the large refrigerated container.

"You see," she told Remo and Chiun, "the big danger of the Ung is that it reproduces so quickly. But that's also its weakness. Dr. Ravits found a pheromone, an attractive scent for the beetles. The canisters will release it and the beetles won't be able to stay away. They'll stop eating, just to reproduce."

"Screwing themselves to death?" Remo said.

"How crude you are," Dara said. "You are the most worthless scientist I ever met."

"Doesn't DDT work?" asked Remo.

"It did. But after a few weeks they built up a resistance to it. Then EDB didn't work. No matter how deadly the toxin, in a short time the Ung is immune to it. It actually feeds on the toxins."

The scientists stumbled through the bugs, getting coatings of the silvery Ung all over themselves as they placed the canisters every ten yards.

Then they ran. The heat of the day would release the scent from the canisters. Some of the scientists stumbled, blinded by the bugs, but when they had all made it back to the cars, the beetles seemed to be gone from them. Still, the very fresh memory of the bugs crawling over them made them slap their bare arms.

Out in the middle of the field there was a hum, dull at first like a whisper and then like a train and then suddenly there appeared to be a writhing hill in the middle of the field. Not only couldn't anyone see the canisters, they couldn't have seen a person anymore if he were standing there.

"It's working, it's working!" cried Dara. She hugged Remo. She liked what she hugged. In joy, one of the scientists hugged everyone around him and hugged Chiun too. He was allowed to escape with multiple abrasions of the arms.

In Korean, Chiun commented that Remo had refused the best offers of Sinanju maidens but now was willing to let himself be publicly disgraced by being fondled and mauled by a passing white.

"I'm still not wearing a kimono, Little Father," said Remo.

When the bugs were densely packed in a hill four stories high, devouring themselves, doors opened briefly from the limousines and the delegates from the countries all over Africa and Asia gathered for the television cameras. Amabasa François Ndo gave a little speech congratulating himself.

Everyone applauded and then returned to the cars and headed back to the airport. All except Ndo. His car rolled up to Remo and Chiun. The door opened and he looked toward Chiun.

Chiun stood motionless. The director general of the IHAEO got out of the car and went to Chiun. Chiun allowed the little wooden god Ga to come from the folds of his kimono, and dropped it into the hands of Ndo.

A television announcer following the Ndo car ordered his cameramen to get the shot of the director general speaking to the man in the kimono and to the scientists.

The announcer spoke into a tape recorder. "After successfully advancing science, the director general stopped to give final instructions to the technicians on how the IHAEO must now keep moving ahead in its relentless struggle against ignorance, disease and famine."

Ndo, like a chubby sneaking a chocolate, secreted the doll in the vest of his suit and was back in the car immediately. The caravan disappeared down the road making giant dust clouds, leaving half-naked natives behind who watched unbelievingly as their dreaded beetle enemy devoured itself in a writhing massive pile.

"I don't know how you two got everybody here, but thank you. Both of you," said Dara, who suddenly realized she was still holding onto the obnoxious one of the pair. She liked holding onto Remo too much.

"One must understand international politics," Chiun said mildly.

"Did you notice it?" Remo suddenly asked Chiun.

"Of course," Chiun said.

"Notice what?" asked Dara.

"A bug," Remo said.

"Bug? There are millions, billions of bugs out there."

Remo nodded. She was right, of course. But there had been another bug and it didn't belong there. It had not been attracted to the pheromone and had flown off crazily toward the hills where the dust now was from the limousines.

In the caravan, Ndo happily toasted the day with Dom Perignon. The guests, all influential delegates from Third World countries, thought Ndo was toasting the success of that peculiar little demonstration in that dirty little village. They all knew he would have to pay for bringing them out here. Some of them had actually missed cocktail parties to be here. And there was no need for it. What had been done was scut work, the kind of thing that white men or Indians or Pakistanis were hired to do. Not delegates. Ndo, they thought, would surely pay.

Ndo did not care what his delegates thought. He would take care of them as he had in the past. He had Ga back, his protector, and when he toasted the day, he toasted not the fight against the Ung beetle, but the return of the Inuti god.

His problems were relieved somewhat by half the delegates being killed on the way to the airport. Ndo, of course, escaped. Ga was with him and this was Inuti land.

9

The delegates who did live to reach their private jets at the national airport could not describe the horrors of the bush. They were glad that some cameramen had been along so their stories would be believed.

They had been attacked by chimpanzees—but not just any chimpanzees.

These ran at them with speeds like motorcycles. These ripped the doors off heavy cars. These crazily smashed their skulls against thick bullet-proof windows. These ate fenders and tore the arms off grown men.

These bent the barrels of guns.

Every delegate knew what was wrong. It was white medicine and First World tampering. The new chemicals used back in the Inuti village had made these normally friendly animals into crazed powerful killers.

The new position of the IHAEO, determined at a caucus in the back of a car, was that IHAEO had developed the part of the chemical that destroyed the Ung beetle. But unfortunately it had been manufactured in a capitalist white factory which had carelessly neglected the environmental concerns so dear to the natural and legitimate inhabitants of the land.

This neglect had led directly to the chimpanzees going berserk. It was all somebody else's fault.

On the planes back, a resolution was passed, over cocktails, praising the delegates for their untiring work toward eradicating famine by their attack on the Ung beetle. The resolution also condemned the greedy manufacturers of the product for failing to take into account its effect on the environment.

The resolution, like all IHAEO resolutions, was passed unanimously. Except this time, there were fewer to be unamimous.

Remo and Chiun had ridden with Dara Worthington and several other scientists in the first ox cart. Up ahead, near the limousine motorcade, they saw dark hairy objects throwing themselves into trees, running around crazed. Up close, they could see a chimpanzee tear off a piece of rock and attempt to eat it. Others slept in a comalike contentment. All along the road were the littered remnants of black limousines, some of the motors still running, some of the air conditioners still making futile little cool puffs into the hot African summer air.

"What is it?" asked Dara.

She saw the remains of one of the delegates who looked as if he had been taken apart, like a chicken sold in pieces.

"I don't know," said one of the scientists in the cart.

They all stopped to examine the creatures. All but Remo and Chiun. Remo was noticing a small object half the size of a fingernail, sitting on a branch that had been denuded of leaves by the recent ravishing of the Ung beetle. Chiun was listening to the researchers.

"Its bones are crushed," said one scientist, holding up the limp hairy limb of a chimp.

Another discovered an extraordinary enlarged heart inside the ripped-open body of another.

In almost every one of the animals, something had been destroyed, or changed.

None of the scientists had ever seen anything like it.

"What on earth happened?" Dara Worthington asked.

While the scientists pored over the remains, Chiun spoke to Remo.

"A chimpanzee, like all other creatures save human beings, uses all its strength. But in this case, look around. It has used more than its strength."

Remo nodded. He knew that he and Chiun were perhaps the only two men on the face of the earth who could use all their strength and power. It was odd, he sometimes thought. He had become more than man by learning to emulate the lower order of creatures.

But the chimps were something else again. They had used all their power, and then more. They had slipped past the regulator built into all animals and used muscles and body parts with so much power that they literally ripped themselves apart or exploded under the strain.

"That's how they killed Dr. Ravits," Remo said. "The cat."

"Exactly," Chiun said.

"Only the cat was inside the room."

"Exactly," Chiun said.

"Nobody could have gotten by you."

"Exactly," said Chiun.

"But something did to the cat what was done to the chimpanzees."

"Exactly," Chiun said.

"Which was why I missed the stroke with that dog in the alley. The dog was infected too."

"No," said Chiun. "You did that because you didn't wear a kimono."

At that moment on the dusty African road, there was satisfaction. Chiun folded his hands delicately into the folds of the sunrise kimono. Remo nodded. They had isolated the problem finally. Now the only questions that remained were how animals could be infected and who would want to do it.

The scientists did not, of course, get to share Remo and Chiun's thinking. Nor were they given the strange thing that Remo had noticed on the branch. It was a simple housefly and it had lain on the branch as if tired. And then, for no reason, it too had quivered and floated off on a hot puff of wind, another small sudden death in a land of vast, violent deaths.

Waldron Perriweather heard about the mass destruction of the Ung beetle near the Inuti village. He heard about the slaughter, the genocide of hundreds of millions of silvery little lives. He wanted to scream; he wanted to infect nurseries; he wanted to drain blood through the skin. He ran to his laboratory and screamed until his eyes almost popped out of his head.

"When, damn it, when?"

"Soon, Mr. Perriweather."

Perriweather buzzed off in a fury. He would have to drive his organization to greater heights.

The Ung beetle had been callously slaughtered, and now it was time to repay that insult.

He had thought that Gloria and Nathan Muswasser might have been helpful but when he had learned that the TNT had been detected before it exploded, he realized he was working with just another pair who were more interested in credit than in doing the work.

"Look," Perriweather had snarled when they

reported their failure. "The movement needs workers, not publicity hounds."

"We were only trying to get credit for the SLA," Gloria had said.

"We're moving beyond credit. We're moving to victory. But before we can win final and ultimate victory, you have got to do your share."

Gloria Muswasser, who had dedicated her life to the revolution, who had struggled without credit, answered back sharply to this rich bourgeois:

"And what's your share? We want to make the world safe for all creatures. And you, you seem animal-insensitive at times. I'm sorry to say it, but it's so."

Nathan nodded.

"I do what I feel like doing," said Perriweather. He had been raised that way.

"Well, we're watching you," Gloria said.

"And I am always watching you," Perriweather had said.

That evening after he had brooded all day over the news of the Ung-beetle disaster, the Muswassers came to Perriweather's home. They seemed absolutely gleeful.

"Why are you smiling?" Perriweather asked.

"More than a hundred delegates are dead. The TNT didn't work but that other thing we planted did."

"Dammit, woman, all the Ung beetles are dead. You think that's a victory?" Perriweather demanded.

"The delegates. More than a hundred. We did it. That thing we planted."

"Where'd you plant it?" Perriweather asked. "Never mind, I'll tell *you*. You planted it inside something refrigerated, didn't you?"

"Right in their refrigerated medicine container," Gloria said with a proud smile.

"Exactly, you idiot. And by the time it had warmed up enough to be of use, it was too late. And all it could do was infect the chimpanzees. The deaths of all those beetles is on your head."

"I'll take the blame for that if I get the credit for the hundred delegates," Gloria said.

Perriweather shook his head. "I can't tolerate this anymore. Now I hear stories about two new scientists at the IHAEO. They say they're preparing even bigger crimes. No more half-measures."

"What are you going to do?" Nathan Muswasser asked.

Perriweather said he was going to take out the entire lab, all its equipment and all its personnel, in retribution for the Ung genocide.

"Impossible," said Gloria.

"Too dangerous," said Nathan.

"You know," Perriweather said coldly, "I've been putting up all the money for the Species Liberation Alliance for years. Every time I'm called on, I defend you, and you people will do anything but take real risks. Now when I need you, where are you? You're telling me things are impossible or too dangerous."

"You're just too interested in bugs," Gloria said.

"And you're just too insensitive to their plight," Perriweather said.

"But we'll work with you," she said. "We need your money, so we'll work with you."

"I think I'll be able to do this one without you," Perriweather said. "If I need you, I'll call."

After they left, he sat for a long while staring at the study door. Of course they didn't understand what he wanted. No one, not since he was five years old, had ever understood what this heir to the Perriweather fortune had wanted.

His wife did not know. He knew what *she* wanted.

She wanted to be married to a Perriweather. Sometimes, she wanted to copulate. Eventually, after being turned down by him enough times, she took lovers. Sometimes he would watch them from the floor above but it just didn't interest him.

He was willing to reproduce. In fact, that had been one of his requirements upon agreeing to marry her. But he insisted that before they copulate, she be with egg.

"I'm not going to fertilize an empty uterus," Waldron had said to the most beautiful debutante of North Shore society, now his bride.

"Well, some people, Waldron, you know, some people enjoy it."

"I guess they do. Some people."

"You didn't tell me you didn't enjoy it," she said.

"You didn't ask," said Waldron, his thin elegant patrician features looking like an ice mask.

"I assumed," she said.

"Not my fault," he said. They had honeymooned on a tour of Europe. Waldron, his bride found out, liked alleys. Garbage dumps held more fascination for him than the Louvre or British theater.

He often mumbled as he passed cemeteries, "Waste. Waste."

"Human life? The death of us all, dear, is inevitable. But we can be remembered by our loved ones," the beautiful young Mrs. Perriweather had said.

"Nonsense," he snarled. "Brass, steel. Airtight, watertight. Just throw them in the ground. Let them do some good."

"Have you always felt this way?" she asked.

"Of course. What a waste. Sealing bodies up like that is so . . . so . . ."

"Futile? Pathetic?" she offered.

"Selfish," said Waldron.

At the time, Perriweather's mother was still living and the young bride asked if Waldron had always been that way.

"You noticed?" asked the grande dame of North Shore society.

"When he asks for rotted fruit for dinner, it really is hard to miss, Mother. May I call you Mother?"

"I'm glad finally that someone does. Yes, Waldron does things that most people might consider different. But he is not, let me stress, he is not insane. Perriweather men have often been different. But they are not, let me reiterate, insane."

The mother-in-law was on her veranda, which stretched out over the rocky line that met the gray Atlantic that fine spring day.

"Perriweather men have sealed themselves in barrels and tried to float down the Amazon. One Perriweather liked to eat roasted bat. Another felt he was the bird god of the Incas, and Waldron's father, I must confess, liked to lather himself in glue before he did 'it.' "

"You poor woman," said the bride.

"Water-soluble. I insisted on water-soluble glue," said the older Mrs. Perriweather. "I never would with epoxy. But back to important things. None of the Perriweather men were ever really insane."

"What does it take for you to call one of them insane?"

"Spending his principal. Failing to live on just the interest on his money. That, my dear, is lunacy. And that is proof that Waldron is not insane because Waldron would never do that."

"I guess there have been worse marriages," the bride said.

"That's what I am telling you, dear."

There really was only one very difficult moment and

that was the night that the doctor told her she was most fertile. Waldron had sex with her as if he didn't want to do any more than light upon her. But it was enough to conceive and carry on the Perriweather name.

After the baby was born, Waldron ignored his wife totally. She complained to her mother-in-law.

"He acts as if I am not his wife," she said.

"The truth is, Waldron does not think that I am his mother," said the old woman.

"I've heard of children wondering who their father was but not their mother. Who does he think is his mother?"

"I don't know. He never tells anyone. He doesn't lie really, he just doesn't talk about it anymore. We have shown him hospital records. Had him talk to the doctor who delivered him. Gotten sworn testimony from nurses. And still, he won't accept me as his mummy."

"Maybe because he was raised by a nanny?" the young woman said.

"All Perriweathers are raised by nannies. I was as affectionate as any mother in the family. But he just wouldn't call me Mom."

"You know what he calls me?" said Waldron's wife.

"What?"

"His egg-layer."

"Dear," said her mother-in-law, sympathetically placing a hand on the young woman's arm. "He never spends the principal."

Waldron Perriweather III not only maintained the Perriweather fortune but he advanced it brilliantly, showing a sense of business that few would expect outside a top management school. It was beyond ruthless. He just seemed to have an inordinate knack for multiplying money rapidly.

He never told his secret but many suspected from
bits and snatches that he simply looked for a chance to
grow on the disasters of others.

What none of them could know was that in learning
to use money, Perriweather had become one of the
more efficient killers on his planet. And he did this as
he invested: without passion; with only a grand
cunning. Money bought services and the difference
between a thug and a surgeon was that a thug usually
gave more thought to tearing somebody apart and was
not so ready with an excuse if he should fail.

Hit men and arm breakers, Waldron found out
early, were far more refreshing to deal with than
doctors. A surgeon might blame death on a patient's
blood pressure and send the bill nevertheless. But a hit
man never charged unless he succeeded.

So in some elements of the underworld, Waldron
Perriweather III was better understood then he was in
his own family or on Wall Street.

Among those who understood him were Anselmo
"Boss" Bossiloni and Myron Feldman, even though
they referred to him between themselves as "that faggy
rich guy."

Anselmo and Myron looked like two cigarette
machines, except that cigarette machines didn't have
hair and, some said, felt more mercy than Anselmo
and Myron. The pair had met in rehabilitation school.
Myron was the better student. He majored in shop and
what he learned was how to use an electric drill
effectively. He found out if you took the drill bit and
put it to someone's kneecap, you could negotiate
anything.

Anselmo majored in gym and learned that if he held
the person down, Myron could work better. They
became inseparable friends. Anselmo was known as

the better-looking one. Anselmo was the one who looked like a Mongolian yak.

When they first met Perriweather, they were working as collectors for loan sharks in Brooklyn. Perriweather offered them more money and strangely asked them if they had strong stomachs. It would have been an even stranger question coming from this elegant dandy if they had not been meeting in a garbage dump where Anselmo and Myron could barely breathe. Perriweather kept talking away, as if he were on a beach somewhere. Anselmo and Myron stayed just long enough to get the name of their first assignment and then left, retching.

The hit was an elderly woman in an estate in Beverly, Massachusetts. They were to break her bones and make it look like a fall.

The way they were to do it made the pair shudder but it was nothing compared to what they found out later. They were not supposed to kill the woman, just break her bones. It was an October morning, the house was enormous and the furniture was all covered with sheets. The house was being closed for the season and the woman thought that they were movers.

Myron and Anselmo had never mugged an elderly woman before and they backed away at first.

"I ain't doing it," they both assured each other. And then the old woman began ordering them around like servants and each found a little place in his heart that said, "Do it."

Her bones were brittle but that was not the hard part. The hard was was leaving her alive, writhing on the floor at the foot of the stairs, begging for help.

Perriweather arrived just as they were leaving.

"Hey, you ain't supposed to be here," Anselmo said. "Whaddaya hire us for if you're gonna be here?"

Perriweather did not answer. He just peeled off the hundred hundred-dollar bills which were their payment and went inside the house, sat down by the poor old woman and began reading a newspaper.

"Waldron," the woman groaned. "I am your mother."

"Are not," Waldron said. "My real mother will be here soon. Now please die so that she will come."

Anselmo looked at Myron and they both shrugged as they left. Later they read that Perriweather had lived in the house for a full week with the body before reporting it to the hospital, which of course notified the police.

At the coroner's inquest, Perriweather testified that he lived in a different wing of the house and had not noticed his mother's body. Apparently she had fallen down the stairs and broken her bones. Servants had left that morning to prepare the family's Florida home and Perriweather thought his mother had gone with them and that he was in the house alone.

"Didn't you smell the body?" the prosecutor had asked. "You could smell that body a half-mile down the road. It was infested with flies. Didn't you wonder what the damned flies were doing in the mansion?"

"Please don't say 'damn,' " Perriweather had said.

A butler and several other servants saved Waldron, however, by testifying that he had a peculiar sense of smell. None at all, they said.

"Why, Mr. Perriweather could be living with a pile of rotted fruit by the bed table for two weeks, smelling so bad you couldn't get a maid into the room with a noseclip."

And there was the recently-estranged Mrs. Perriweather who admitted that her husband had a fondness for garbage dumps.

There was also testimony that there was no one who could have smelled the rotting corpse because the last two in the house, other than Mr. Perriweather, were brutal-looking movers in a white Cadillac.

Accidental death was the verdict. The prosecutor said Perriweather should go and have his nose fixed.

Anselmo and Myron had more work from Perriweather over the years. They also knew he hired others but they weren't sure who and sometimes he would complain about amateur help. Sometimes he would say strange things too. Anselmo couldn't remember how the topic of their first job for him came up but he did hear Perriweather mention that his true mother visited him a day after the first hit had been made.

A nut case, they both decided, but the money was good and none of the jobs were dangerous because Perriweather always had them well planned. So when he called and told them he wanted them to steal an atomic device, there was no complaint, especially since he had agreed to meet them out in the open, in the fresh air.

He was mumbling something about revenge and they had never seen him this angry.

But his plans were again good. He showed them pictures of the atomic installation and gave them the proper passwords to use and badges to wear.

"Ain't that stuff radio-whatever?" asked Anselmo. He had read about those things.

"Radioactive," Perriweather said. "You won't have to handle it long. You just give it to these two people." And he showed them a picture of a young woman with a blank expression and a young man with eyes that wimped out to the world.

"Those are the Muswassers. They'll plant the device. Tell them not to worry about getting it inside the gate this time. It doesn't have to be inside the gate. That's the beauty of the atomic device, you only have to be within a mile or so of your target. The one thing I do want, though, and tell them to be sure to do this, is to get these two in the laboratory when they set off the device."

Waldron showed his hit men a picture of two men, one wearing a kimono, the other a thin white man with thick wrists.

"I want them dead," Perriweather said.

"How should these other two make sure they're inside?" asked Myron.

"I don't know. You do it. You tell them when you set it off. I am tired of dealing with amateurs."

"Mr. Perriweather, can I ask a personal question?" asked Anselmo, venturing a familiarity that years of good business cooperation had granted him.

"What is it?"

"Why do you use amateurs in the first place anyway?"

"Sometimes, Anselmo, one has no choice. You are stuck with your allies, no matter how temporary."

"I see," said Anselmo.

"That's why I really like dealing with you, though," Perriweather said. "There's only one thing wrong with the two of you."

"What's that?"

"You both have nice hair. Why do you wash it so much?"

"You mean it takes the life out of it?"

"No. Removes the food," said Perriweather.

As always, Anselmo and Myron found Perriweather's plans were perfect. They were able to get into the nuclear storage facility with absolute ease and escape with the two packages, one containing the weapon and the other the timing detonator.

They met Nathan and Gloria Muswasser at a town house outside Washington. Nathan's father owned it. The fine plastered walls were covered with liberation posters. They called for freeing the oppressed, for saving animals. There was a special call for freeing blacks.

Apparently this had already been achieved because the entire neighborhood was free of blacks.

"Youse got to be careful of these things," Anselmo said. "And you shouldn't set it off until these two guys is in the lab."

"Which two guys?" Gloria asked.

Anselmo showed them the photograph of the Oriental and the white.

"How will we know they are in there?"

"We'll tell you."

"All right. Seems simple. Fair enough," Gloria said. "Now to the important part. Who gets the credit?"

"No credit. We don't deal in credit. But we already been paid."

"Wait a minute. We're going to be doing the lab, maybe two hundred people, the surrounding suburbs, add at least ten to fifteen thousand people there . . . Nathan, remember we've got to try to figure out a way to get the pets out of the area if we can. We're really talking about fifteen thousand people. Maybe twenty."

Anselmo shuddered at the potential death toll. Even Myron's dull brain registered a glimmer of horror.

"So we want to know," Gloria said, "just where you stand on the credit."

"We been paid."

"I'm talking about taking credit for the bombing."

"What?" said both men in unison.

"Credit. We may have twenty thousand dead here. Who gets credit for it?"

"You mean blame?"

"That's unprogressive. I am talking about credit for the act. Publicity."

"If it's okay with you, girlie, you can have all the credit," Anselmo said.

"We'll give you alternate credit. We can say you assisted us. But the main cause is ours. The SLA takes full credit for this one."

"You don't even have to mention us, girlie."

"You sure now? We may be going as high as twenty-five thousand deaths here. You don't want any part of it?"

"No, no. That's okay," Myron said. "In fact, don't mention us at all. Ever. Never. No way."

"That's downright selfless of you," Gloria said. "Nathan, I like these people."

"Then why are they doing it?" Nathan said. He looked at Anselmo. "If you're not getting credit, why steal a bomb? Why all the trouble?"

"We get paid, kid," Anselmo said.

"You're doing it for the money?"

"Damned right."

"Why go to all this trouble for money? I mean, where is your daddy?" Nathan asked.

Myron and Anselmo looked at each other again.

"Nathan means you could get the money from your fathers," Gloria said.

"You don't know our fathers," said Myron.

"Never mind. You're sure you don't even want an 'assisted by' and then your names?"

"No. We don't want anything," Myron said.

"And be sure," Anselmo said, "that you don't set that thing off until we say so, okay?"

"Sure. Maybe we don't understand all your reasons, but I want you to know I sense solidarity with you. That we are all part of the same struggle," Nathan said.

"Sure. But don't set that thing off until we say so."

10

"Must we stay in this rat cage again?" Chiun asked.

"Sorry, Little Father," Remo said. "But until we find out what's going on with these labs, we stay here."

"Easy enough for you to say, fat white thing. There is so much suet on your body that you can be comfortable sleeping on hard floors. But I? I am delicate. My frail body requires real rest."

"You're as delicate as granite," Remo said.

"Don't worry, Chiun," said Dara Worthington.

"You know that I am reduced to spending my life with him and you tell me not to worry?" Chiun said.

"No, it's just that we have rooms here in the laboratory complex. I'll get them to fix one up for you. A real bedroom. One for you too," she said to Remo.

"A real bedroom?" Chiun asked, and Dara nodded.

"With a television set?"

"Yes."

"Would it have one of those tape-playing machines?" Chiun asked.

"As a matter of fact, yes."

"Would you by any chance have a complete set of tapes from the show *As the Planet Revolves?*" Chiun asked.

"Afraid not," she said. "That show hasn't been on the air for ten years."

"Savages," Chiun mumbled in Korean to Remo. "You whites are all savages and philistines."

"She's doing the best she can, Chiun," Remo answered in Korean. "Why don't you just get off everybody's back for a while?"

Chiun raised himself to his full height. "That is a despicable thing to say, even for you," he said in Korean.

"I didn't think it was so bad," Remo said.

"I will not speak to you again until you apologize."

"Hell will freeze over first," Remo said.

"What language is that?" Dara said. "What are you two saying?"

"That was real language," Chiun said. "Unlike the dog barkings that pass for language in this vile land."

"Chiun was just thanking you for the offer of the bedroom," Remo said.

"You're welcome, Dr. Chiun," Dara said with a large smile.

In Korean again, Chiun grumbled: "The woman is too stupid even to insult. Like all whites."

"Are you talking to me?" Remo asked.

Chiun folded his arms and turned his back on Remo.

"Sticks and stones may break my bones, but being ignored will never hurt me," Remo said.

"Stop teasing that sweet man," Dara said.

She settled them into adjoining rooms in one of the wings of the IHAEO building.

Remo was lying on his back on the small cot, looking up at the ceiling, when there was a faint tap on the door.

He called out and Dara entered.

"I just wanted to see if you were comfortable," she said.

"I'm fine."

She came into the room, shyly at first, but when Remo said nothing, she strode forward and sat on a chair next to his bed.

"I guess I'm still crashing from everything that happened today," she said. "It was glorious and it was awful too."

"I know," Remo said. "I always feel that way about transatlantic flights."

"I don't mean that," she said. She leaned over toward him. "I mean what we did with the Ung beetle. That was glorious and it will live forever. But then, oh, those poor men, when those apes attacked. It was awful."

Remo said nothing and Dara lowered her face toward his so she was staring evenly into his eyes. Her breasts brushed across his chest. She wore no brassiere.

"Wasn't it awful?"

"That's the tits," he said. "I mean, the truth. It was awful."

"I never saw such crazed animals," she said.

"Umm" Remo said. He liked the feel of her against him.

"There are no bad animals, you know. Something made them that way."

"Um," Remo said.

"I'm glad you were there to protect me," Dara said.

"Umm," Remo said.

"What could have caused that?" she asked.

"Ummm."

"What kind of an answer is that?"

"I mean, I'll look into it in the morning," Remo said.

"But what do you think?" she persisted.

What Remo thought was that the only way he was going to keep her quiet was to do something physical, so he put his arms around her and pulled her body down onto his. She instantly glued her mouth to his in a long tender kiss.

"I've been thinking of that all day," she said.

"I know," Remo said, reaching over and pulling the chain that turned off the small night lamp.

The FBI no longer guarded the laboratories so the only security was a tired old guard inside a wooden shack at the front gate.

Anselmo and Myron drove up in their white Cadillac and Anselmo lowered the driver's window.

"What can I do for you?" the guard said.

Anselmo held up a white box that was on the front seat alongside him.

"Pizza delivery," he said.

"Pretty fancy pizza wagon," the guard said, nodding at the Cadillac limousine.

"Well, I usually got a big pizza slice on top of the car, but I take it off at night. The kids, you know."

"Yeah, kids are bastards, ain't they?" the guard said.

"Sure are."

"Go ahead through," the guard said. "You can park in the lot up there."

"We're looking for Dr. Remo and Dr. Chiun. You know where they are?"

The guard looked at a list on a clipboard. "They came in earlier with everybody else and they didn't sign out. But I don't know what lab they're in."

"But they're in there, right?"

"Have to be," the guard said. "No way out except past me, and no one's gone out tonight."

"Maybe they're sleeping," Anselmo said.

"Maybe," the guard said.

"Maybe I won't disturb them. I'll tell you what. You take the pizza and we'll let them rest."

"Does it have anchovies?" the guard asked.

"No. Just extra cheese and pepperoni," Anselmo said.

"I like anchovies best," the guard said.

"The next time, I bring you one with anchovies," Anselmo promised.

"Won't those two doctors be mad?" the guard asked.

"Not as mad as they're gonna be later," Anselmo said. He shoved the pizza into the guard's hands, put the Cadillac in reverse and slid away. "Don't forget the anchovies," the guard called.

Two blocks away, Anselmo parked alongside a telephone booth and called the Muswassers' number.

"Yes?" Gloria said.

"They're at the lab," Anselmo said.

"Good. We're all ready."

"Just give us time to get out of town," Anselmo said.

Gloria Muswasser crawed through the manicured greenery of the IHAEO laboratory complex. She was wearing Earth shoes and a filthy green combat uniform which she had treasured ever since she rolled a Vietnam vet for it in 1972.

Her husband trailed along behind her, emitting little squeaks of pain as bits of rock and twigs scratched his flaccid abdomen.

"Why did I have to come along anyway?" Nathan whined. "You're carrying the whole thing by yourself. You didn't need me."

"No, I didn't," Gloria snapped in agreement. "But I figured if we got caught, I wouldn't have to go to jail alone."

He grabbed her ankle. "Is there a chance of getting caught?"

"None at all, if you keep quiet," she said.

"I don't want to go to jail," Nathan said.

"We won't. I promise you. Before I let the establishment pigs take you, Nathan, I'll gun you down myself."

Nathan gulped.

"It'll make all the papers. You'll be a martyr to the cause."

"That's . . . that's groovy, Gloria."

"Don't say 'groovy.' It's out-of-date. Say 'awesome.' "

"Okay. It's awesome, Gloria."

"Totally," she agreed. "Also incredible."

"Yeah. That too," Nathan said.

"How about here?" she said. She pointed to a spot of turf near a mulberry bush.

"Totally incredible, Gloria."

"Good. We'll plant the damn thing right here."

"Like a flower," Nathan said. "We'll plant it like a flower. Remember flowers? You used to be real into flowers."

"Screw flowers. Flowers never got us anywhere. Violence is where we're coming from now. Nobody ever gave up shit because of flowers."

"Yeah. Up flowers. Violence is where it's at."

"Don't say 'where it's at,' Nathan. It's out-of-date. Say 'bottom line.' "

"Bottom line?"

"Violence is the bottom line," Gloria said, as she turned the time for 120 minutes. "She's going to go, baby."

"Should we watch?"

"Of course not, asshole. We'd be blown up. We'll call the television stations. *They'll* watch."

"They'll be blown up too," Nathan said.

"Serves them right," she said. "And that's the bottom line."

"Groovy," Nathan said.

Gloria slapped him behind the ear as they crawled away through the dark.

Forty-five minutes later, a television crew showed up at the IHAEO ground and found a large hole cut in the wire safety fence, exactly where the anonymous telephone callers had said it would be.

"This better be good," the head cameraman for WIMP said.

His assistant looked toward the white lab buildings looming in the background behind the fence.

"What are we waiting for?" he asked.

"What else? For Rance Renfrew, hard-hitting television newsman, the man who tells it like it is, your man from WIMP."

Both cameramen chuckled at the imitation of the station's commercial.

"Does he know what it is?" the assistant cameraman said.

"Nope."

"I can't wait to see the look in his eyes."

"Me neither."

They waited a half-hour before a black limousine pulled up in front of them and a young man so brimful of good health that even his hair looked suntanned stepped out of the back. He was wearing a tuxedo and he growled at the two cameramen. "This better be important. I was at a big dinner."

"It is," the head cameraman said, winking toward his assistant. "Some group is planning a big protest here tonight."

"Protest? You got me away from a dinner for a protest? What kind of protest?"

"Something to save animals," the cameraman said. "And protest American genocide."

"Well, that sounds better," Rance Renfrew said. "We could get something good here." He rehearsed his voice like a musician tuning an instrument. "This is Rance Renfrew on the scene where a group of enraged Americans tonight attacked their government's genocidal policies toward . . ." He looked at the cameramen: "You said animals?"

"Right, animals."

"Their government's genocidal policies toward animals. Could this be the beginning of a movement that will topple down corrupt American governments forever? Not bad. That might work. When's the demonstration supposed to be anyway?"

"About another forty-five minutes or so," the cameraman said.

"Well, we'll be ready. We'll get filmed and say we left a private party to come here to bring our viewers the truth. What are they going to do anyway?"

"Set off an atomic bomb, they said."

The suntan vanished and Rance Renfrew's skin turned pale. "Here?" he said.

"That's what they said."

"Listen, fellas. I think I've got to get some more equipment. You wait here and film anything that happens and I'll be back."

"What kind of equipment do you need?"

"I think I need a muffle on this mike. It's been making my voice too harsh."

"I've got one in the gadget bag," the cameraman said.

"And I need a blue shirt. This white glares too much."

"I've got one of those too."

"And new shoes. I need a different pair of shoes if I'm going to be traipsing around. These are too tight. I'll go get them. You wait for me and film whatever happens."

"Okay. How long will you be?"

"I don't know. My best shoes are at my weekend apartment."

"Where's that?"

"In Miami. But I'll try to get back as soon as I can."

Renfrew jumped into the limousine and speeded away. Behind him, the two cameramen broke into guffaws and finally the assistant said, "Hey, shouldn't we be a little worried too? I mean, they said an atomic bomb."

"Come on. These assholes couldn't blow up a firecracker on the Fourth of July," the head cameraman said.

"I guess you're right. Should we warn anybody inside the complex? You know, bomb scare or whatever?"

"No, let them sleep. Nothing's going to happen except maybe some noisy pickets."

"Then what the hell are we here for?" the assistant asked.

"For time and a half after eight hours. What did you think?"

"Got it."

Inside Remo's room, the telephone rang, and without thinking, Dara Worthington reached out a satisfied limp hand toward the receiver.

"Oops," she caught herself. "Maybe I shouldn't."

"You'd better not," Remo said. "It's for me."

"How do you know?"

"There's somebody who always calls me when I'm having a good time. He's got an antenna for it. I think he's afraid I might OD on happiness so he's saving me from a terrible fate." He held the phone to his ear.

"Your dime," he said.

"Remo," Smith's lemony tones echoed. "It's—"

"Yeah, yeah, Aunt Mildred," said Remo, using one of the code names with which Smith signed messages.

"This is serious. Are you alone?"

"Enough," Remo said vaguely.

"There's been a serious robbery," Smith said.

"I'm already on a case," Remo said.

"It may be the same case," Smith said. "This was a robbery from a nuclear installation. The missing object is a micronic component fission-pack and a detonator."

"Does anybody who speaks English know what was stolen?" Remo asked.

"That means a small portable nuclear weapon and the means to set it off."

"Well, what can I do about it?"

"The thieves weren't seen so we don't know anything about them," Smith said. "But I've just gotten word that some press organizations received threats tonight aimed against the IHAEO lab."

"Aha. The plot thickens," Remo said. "What does it all boil down to?"

"If it explodes, the bomb could destroy all animal and plant life for twenty square miles," Smith said. "Not to mention the catastrophic effect on the environment."

"Tell me. If it blows, will it get the House of Representatives?" Remo asked.

"Without question."

"I think maybe I should go back to sleep," Remo said.

"This is serious," Smith said.

"Okay, I get the picture." Remo slid past Dara Worthington and slipped into his trousers. "I'll look around. Anything else?"

"I should think that would be enough," Smith said.

Remo hung up and patted Dara on her bare hindquarters.

"Sorry, darling. Something's come up."

"Again? So soon? How lovely."

"Work," Remo said. "Just sit tight."

"Your Aunt Mildred sounds very demanding," Dara said. "I heard you call her that."

"She is," Remo said. "She is." He wondered if he should tell her about the bomb threat but decided not to. If he couldn't find the bomb, there wasn't much chance of anyone living anyway.

Remo went into the next room where Chiun lay in the middle of the floor in the thin blanket stripped from the apartment bed.

"Not asleep, Little Father?" Remo asked.

"Sleep? How does one sleep when one's ears are besieged by the sounds of rutting moose next door?"

"Sorry, Little Father. It was just something that happened."

"Anyway, I am not speaking to you," Chiun said, "so I would appreciate your moving your bleached noisy carcass out of my room."

"In a little while, none of us may be talking to anybody," Remo said. "There may be a bomb on the grounds."

Chiun said nothing.

"A nuclear bomb."

Chiun was silent.

"I'll do it myself, Chiun," said Remo. "But I don't know much about how to find a bomb. If I don't find it and we all get blown to kingdom come, I just want you to know, well, that it was wonderful knowing you."

Chiun sat up and shook his head. "You are hopelessly white," he said.

"What's my color got to do with it?"

"Everything. Only a white man would search for a bomb by trying to locate a bomb," Chiun said as he rose and brushed past Remo and led the way outdoors.

Remo followed and said, "It sounds reasonable to me, searching for a bomb by looking for a bomb. What would you look for? A four-leaf clover and hope to get lucky?"

"I," the aged Korean said loftily, "would look for tracks. But then I am only a poor abused gentle soul, not nearly so worldly wise as you are."

"What do bomb tracks look like?"

"You don't look for bomb tracks, you imbecile. You look for people tracks. Unless the bomb delivered itself here, people tracks will be left by those who carried it."

"Okay. Let's look for people tracks," Remo said. "And thank you for talking to me."

"You're welcome. Will you promise to wear a kimono?"

"I'd rather not find the bomb," Remo said.

TV station WIMP's chief competitor in the ratings, station WACK, had just arrived on the scene in the person of a camera crew and Lance Larew, anchorman who was, if anything, even tanner than Rance Renfrew, his main rival in the news rating race.

He saw the two cameramen from WIMP but felt elated when he did not see Rance Renfrew around.

"All right, men," he said. "Let's set up and shoot." He took a portable toothbrush from inside his tuxedo pocket and quickly brushed his teeth.

A cameraman said to him, "Hey, if a bomb's gonna go off here, I don't want to be around."

"This is where the action is, boy, and where the action is, you'll find Lance Larew and station WACK."

"Yeah, well the action may be five miles up in the air pretty soon if there's a bomb and it goes off."

"Don't worry. We'll shoot our stuff and get out of here," Larew said. "Let's get in on the grounds."

"I think I see something," Remo said.

Standing on the smooth, damp turf on the lawn, Remo pointed to a series of small impressions following a snaking line. "The grass is flattened here. A combat crawl," he said.

"Amateurs," Chiun said with disdain. He pointed to a small indentation. "Right-handed. Even her elbows leave prints."

"Her?" Remo said.

"Obviously a woman's elbow," Chiun said.

"Obviously," said Remo.

"With a man following behind her. But the woman was carrying the device," Chiun said.

"Obviously," Remo said.

"Hey, look," Lance Larew hissed to his cameramen. "I think there's somebody up ahead. Who are those guys?"

"Maybe they're scientists," the cameraman said.

"Maybe. Let's roll the cameras and stay with them in case they blow up."

They were talking in whispers but fifty yards away,

Chiun turned to Remo and said, "Who are these noisy fools?"

"I don't know. First the bomb, then I'll take care of them." He looked down at the tracks. "I think you're onto something."

"He's onto something," one of the camera crew shouted. He lumbered forward with his equipment. Lance Larew followed him.

"Perhaps I should dispatch these meddlers into the void," Chiun said, "so we may continue our search in peace."

"Oh, I don't know," Remo said. "Kill a newsman and you never hear the end of it."

"I don't like performing in front of these louts, like a circus elephant."

"Let me find the bomb first," Remo said. He followed the line of the tracks to a flowering bush. He felt the ground with his fingers. The device was there, covered scantily by a coating of earth.

"Hurry. They are encroaching," Chiun whispered as the newsmen came closer. Finally, one of the cameramen pushed forward quickly and flicked his camera in Chiun's direction. Chiun pressed his nose against the lens.

"Hey, cut it out, Methuselah," the cameraman said. "You're getting nose grease all over my lens."

"Nose grease? The Master of Sinanju does not produce nose grease. You have insulted me to the core of my being."

"Now you've done it," Remo called out. "I'm not responsible anymore."

"What is it you're doing there?" Lance Larew shouted. "What are you doing under that bush?"

Remo's hands worked fast, first disconnecting the timer, and then dismembering the nuclear device by pounding the metal pieces into powder. He buried the little pile of black and silver granules beneath the mulberry bush.

"I said what are you doing there?" Larew said. He was standing near Remo now.

"Looking for the dreaded Australian night-stalker," Remo said. "This is the only night it blooms. But we missed it. We'll have to wait until next year."

"What about the bomb?" Larew demanded.

"There was no bomb," Remo said. "We've been getting calls like that for weeks. Just cranks."

"You mean I came all this way on a crank call?" Larew said.

"Seems like it," Remo said.

Larew stamped his foot in anger, then called to the two cameramen behind him. "All right, men. We'll do a feature story anyway. Scientists prowl the grounds at midnight looking for a rare flower."

"You don't want to do that," Remo said.

"Don't tell me what I want to do," Larew said. "First Amendment rights. Freedom of the press. Free speech." He turned to the cameramen. "Shoot some footage on these guys."

The two cameramen aimed at Remo and Chiun, and began rolling the tapes inside the devices.

Chiun's narrow hazel eyes peered into one of the cameras.

"How about a little smile?" the cameraman said.

"Like this?" Chiun asked, his face contorted in a strained smile.

"That's good, old man. More teeth."

Chiun grabbed the camera and, still smiling, crushed it into a flat slab. Bowing, he handed it back to the cameraman. "Enough teeth?" he asked.

Remo grabbed the other camera from the other

cameraman and shredded it into noodle-shaped pieces.

"First Amendment!" screamed Larew.

Remo put some of camera pieces into Larew's mouth. "First Amendment that," he said.

The news crew fled toward the rip in the chain-link fence.

"Thank you, Chiun, for your help," Remo said.

"Will you . . . ?"

"I still won't wear a kimono," Remo said.

Gloria Muswasser's ear was getting tired. She cradled the telephone between her head and her shoulder while on a piece of blue paper she crossed out another set of television call letters.

She dialed another number.

"WZRO newsroom," a male voice said.

"I am the spokesman for the Species Liberation Alliance," Gloria said in her most menacing terrorist voice.

"So?"

"I am calling to claim credit for the near-holocaust at the IHAEO labs tonight."

"What holocaust? What near-holocaust? The biggest news tonight is that the President's sleeping soundly with no bad dreams."

"It was nearly a holocaust," Gloria insisted.

"Nearly doesn't count."

"What are you talking about? We almost blew the Eastern Seaboard back to the Stone Age."

"Almost doesn't count either," the bored voice on the telephone said.

"Now you listen, you military industrial pig sympathizer," Gloria shouted. "We are the SLA and we mean to claim credit for an atomic blast that would have made Hiroshima look like a fart in a bottle. The holocaustal potential for this is staggering."

"I don't care if you're the SLA, the A.F.of L. of the S-H-I-T-S," the newsman said. "Nothing happened tonight, so there's no news."

"Jesus," Gloria sighed. "Nothing happened. Always you want action. You're sensationalist scandal-mongers."

"That's about it," the newsman said.

"Disgusting."

"If you say so," he agreed.

"Doesn't intent count for anything?"

"Lady," the newsman said tiredly. "If malicious intent were the basis for a story, the evening news would be forty hours long."

"But this was a freaking atomic bomb, you asshole," Gloria screamed.

"And this is a dial tone," the newsman said as he hung up on her.

Gloria lit a cigarette from the butt of Nathan's.

"We've got to come up with a new plan," she said.

"They didn't buy it?"

"Pigs. The guy said malicious intent wasn't enough."

"It was enough in Vietnam," Nathan said in his most self-righteous tone.

"What the hell is that supposed to mean?" Gloria asked.

"I don't know," Nathan said mildly. "Talking about Vietnam is usually safe."

"Vietnam isn't in anymore," Gloria said, "so stop jerking around. This is important. Perriweather's going to hit the ceiling when he finds out the bomb didn't go off. He must have spent a fortune on this."

"A fortune," Nathan said. Agreeing with Gloria was almost always safe.

"Maybe we can come up with something just as good. Something sensational that the media would be interested in," Gloria said.

"WIMP wasn't interested?" Nathan asked.

"They said they sent a crew but everybody went home."

"And WACK?" Nathan asked.

"They sent a crew too and got assaulted by some people watching flowers bloom. So we've got to come up with something good."

"Like what?"

"Think," Gloria demanded.

Nathan pressed his eyebrows together. "How's this?"

"That's real good," she said.

"I'm thinking. How about a protest?"

"Protests are out," she said. "It's got to be big."

"We used to liberate banks," Nathan said.

"No good. Banks are out too."

"What's in?"

"Schools and supermarkets," Gloria said. "Stuff like that. Murdering children is always good."

"How about a hospital," Nathan said. "Or is that too gross?"

"A hospital?" Gloria said sharply.

"Yeah. Really, I didn't mean it the way it sounded."

"That's brilliant. A hospital. A children's ward. And we'll do it on those days when they bring pets to play with kids. We'll show them to let the little bastards mistreat animals."

"Real good," Nathan said. "Right on."

"Don't say that. 'Right on' is out."

"Sorry, Gloria. I meant your idea is really the bottom line."

"It's the max," she said.

"Real max, Gloria," said Nathan.

"Good. Now we can call Perriweather and tell him what we're planning," Gloria said. "I was never too hot on that atomic-bomb idea anyway."

"Too destructive?" Nathan said.

"Naaah, but who'd be around to notice the blood?" Gloria asked.

11

Dr. Dexter Morley was sitting on a high stool, his pudgy cheeks flushed, his fat little fingers clasped together in his lap, when Perriweather entered the lab. The little scientist's lips curved into a prideful quick grin when he saw his employer.

"Well?" Perriweather asked impatiently.

"The experiment is complete," Morley said. His voice quivered with excitement and accomplishment.

"Where is it?" Perriweather asked, brushing past the scientist and heading for the lab tables.

"There are two of them," Morley said, trying frantically and futilely to keep Perriweather's hands off the sterile surfaces in the lab. "If you'll just wait a moment . . ."

"I've waited enough moments," Perriweather snapped. "Where?"

Dr. Morley stiffened at the rebuke but went to get a small cheesecloth-covered box on a shelf. As his hands touched it, they trembled. "Here," he said, his voice hushed and filled with awe as he removed the cloth.

Beneath it was a Plexiglas cube. Inside the cube was a piece of rotting meat. Sitting on top of the meat, feeding and lazily twitching, were two red-winged flies.

"A breeding pair?" Perriweather asked. "You got a breeding pair?"

"Yes, Mr. Perriweather."

Involuntarily, Perriweather gasped at the sight of the flies. He lifted the plastic cube with hands so gentle that the flies never moved from the piece of meat. He watched them from every angle, turning the cube this way and that, observing them from below and above and eye-to-eye, marveling at the stained-glass redness of their wings.

"Their wings are exactly the color of fresh human blood," he whispered.

As he watched, the two flies rose from the meat and briefly coupled in the air before settling back down.

Almost to himself, Perriweather said, "If I could only find a woman who could do that."

For some reason, Dr. Dexter Morley felt vaguely embarrassed, like a Peeping Tom caught in the act. He cleared his throat and said, "Actually, the two flies are exactly like ordinary houseflies, except for the color of the wings. *Musca domestica* of the order Diptera."

"They're not exactly like houseflies," said Perriweather, casting a sharp glance at the scientist. "You didn't change that, did you?"

"No. No, I didn't."

"Then it's the ultimate life form," Perriweather said slowly, rotating the plastic cube as if it were a flawless blue-white diamond that he had just found in his backyard.

"Well, I wouldn't go that far," Dr. Morley said, fluttering his eyelids and attempting a weak smile.

"What would you know?" Perriweather hissed.

"Uh. Yes, sir. What I was about to say was that in most respects the species is an ordinary housefly. Shape and structure. Its eating habits are the same, which unfortunately makes it a disease bearer, although I believe that in time we could eliminate—"

"Why would you want to eliminate that?" Perriweather said.

"What? Its disease-bearing properties?"

Perriweather nodded.

"Why . . ." The scientist shook his head. "Perhaps we are not communicating, Mr. Perriweather. Flies do bear disease."

"Of course. If they didn't, there would be even more humans on earth today than we've already got."

"I . . . er, I guess I see your point," Morley said. "I think. But still, *Musca morleyalis* is still a disease bearer and therefore dangerous."

"*Musca morleyalis?*" Perriweather asked. His face was expressionless.

Morley flushed. "Well, generally, discoveries such as these are attributed to the scientist who . . ."

Perriweather's face still showed no expression as he said, "Try *Musca Perriweatheralis.*" Finally his face broke into a small smile.

The scientist cleared his throat. "Very well," he said softly.

"Why are their wings red?" Perriweather asked.

"Ah." The scientist flushed. He was more comfortable talking about biology than disputing names with his terrifying employer. "The amino acids developed in this species are, as I said, radically different from the ordinary housefly's. Not only in type, but in location. Apparently, that produced the genetic mutation that gave us the red wings. Naturally, when the experiments continue and we destroy these particular organisms, then we'll start to relocate the—"

"Destroy? Destroy what?" Perriweather's eyes blazed.

"Since we have all the paperwork, it really isn't

necessary to keep the actual organisms, particularly since their respiratory systems are developed to a point that makes them incompatible with other forms of life."

"Meaning?"

"Meaning that these flies are immune to DDT, other pesticides and all poisons," Morley said. "That was the point, wasn't it?"

"That was exactly the point," Perriweather said. His eyes sparkled. "All pesticides?"

"All pesticides currently known. Allow me." He lifted the plastic cube from Perriweather's hands and placed it on the gleaming white lab table. Wearing rubber gloves, he inserted the gauze flycatcher into the box and withdrew one of the flies. Next he opened a small container from which a soft hiss issued. "Pure DDT," Morley said as he lowered the flycatcher into the container and closed the top.

"What's going to happen?" Perriweather asked anxiously.

"Absolutely nothing," Morley said. "There's enough pure pesticide in that—"

"Please don't refer to them as pesticides," Perriweather said.

"Sorry, there's enough DDT in there to kill a country full of flies. But notice the condition of *Musca perriweatheralis.*" He pulled out the gauze flycatcher and covered the top of the box. Inside the gauze, the red-winged fly buzzed angrily. When he placed it back into the plastic cube, it darted straight for the piece of meat.

"He's still alive," Perriweather said.

"And unharmed," Morley added. "It can survive in an atmosphere of pure methane," the scientist said proudly. "Or cyanide. Or any poison you can think of."

"Then it's invincible."

"That's why it has to be destroyed," Morley said. "I'm sure you wouldn't want to risk having a creature like this loose in our atmosphere," he said. "As it is, the precautions I've taken with it have been enormous. But the danger grows as the pair breeds. If even one such fly gets out of this lab alive, it could significantly jeopardize the ecological balance of the planet."

"A fly that can't be poisoned," Perriweather said proudly.

"As you know, Mr. Perriweather, it is much more than that. There are the other things it does. Its ability to bite, for instance, unlike *Musca domestica.* And the result of its bites. You know, Mr. Perriweather, when I first came here to work, you promised that one day you would tell me how you had developed those initial mutations."

"Let's see the demonstration again," Perriweather said. Morley noticed that his employer was breathing hard.

"Must we?"

"We must," Perriweather said. His voice was a soft uninflected drone, almost like a buzz, but it chilled Morley more than shouting would have.

"Very well."

The scientist went to a far corner of the lab to a terrarium filled with salamanders. He took one out and brought it back to the plastic cube containing the flies.

"You be careful. I don't want that lizard accidentally eating one of those flies."

"It won't," Morley said. He covered the salamander's head and held it inside the container with the flies. One of the flies lighted on the salamander's tail for a second, then hopped back onto the lump of rancid meat.

Morley tossed the salamander into another clear
plastic container that already held a large wood frog.
The frog was a dozen times larger than the lizard; its
body weight must have been one hundred times as
great. The frog looked at the salamander and flicked
out a lazy tongue.

Perriweather moved up next to the plastic cube; his
face touched it as he watched to see what would
happen next.

The frog flicked out its tongue again and almost
instantly its tongue had been severed and was lying on
the bottom of the container, still twitching reflexively.
The frog's eyes bulged in terror as the salamander
attacked it, biting it fiercely, and ripped off large
chunks of skin from its body. Then the lizard grabbed
and ripped the limbs from the frog. The frog's eyes
burst into blobs of jelly. Its clear-colored blood
sprayed against the plastic sides of the container. It
made a feeble sound; then its resonating cavities were
filled with its own bodily fluids. The frog twitched,
and then lay immobile on the floor of the cage, as the
tiny salamander crawled atop it, still attacking.

Another two more minutes, the interior of the
plastic container was invisible from the outside. The
frog's entrails and fluids had covered the sides. Silently
Dr. Morley lifted the top of the box and inserted a long
hypodermic needle and withdrew it with the dead
salamander impaled on the tip.

"Air injected right into the heart," he said, tossing
the reptile into a plastic bag. "Only way I know to kill
it."

He looked at Perriweather. "Now you see why these
two must be destroyed?"

Perriweather looked at the flies for a long time
before looking back to the scientist.

"I'll take care of it," Perriweather said. "For the time being, guard them with your life."

The room upstairs was dark, as it always was, and hot, and smelled of sweetness and rot. Waldron Perriweather III entered quietly, as he always did, carefully replacing the key in his jacket pocket after unlocking the door. The dust in the room lay in sheets across the ancient velvet furniture with delicate crocheted doilies.

Perriweather walked softly across the dusty threadbare rug to a high mantel covered with antique silk. On top of the silk was only one object, a tiny jeweled case thickly crusted with gold and precious stones.

Lovingly he picked up the case and held it for several minutes in the palm of his hand. He stared at it, not speaking, not moving, except for the gentle strokes of his fingers upon its jeweled surface.

Finally, taking a deep breath, he opened the case.

Inside lay the tiny corpse of a fly.

Perriweather's eyes softened with a film of tears. With a trembling finger, he touched the hairy, still little body.

"Hello, Mother."

12

Perriweather was back at the desk in his study when the telephone rang.

"Mr. Perriweather," Gloria Muswasser said. "We're sorry but the bomb didn't go off."

When she got off the telephone, she would tell Nathan that Perriweather didn't seem to mind at all. He was cordial. More than cordial.

"It wasn't our fault either," Gloria said. "The fuckup was due to the paranoid insensitivity of the unenlightened news media and—"

"No matter, Mrs. Muswasser," Perriweather said. "I have contingency plans."

"So do we," Gloria said, thinking of the children's ward at the hospital. "Nathan and I just came up with something so fantastic, so big, you're going to really love it."

"I'm sure I will," Perriweather said. "Why don't you come out to the house and tell me about it?"

"Really? Really? You're not mad?"

"Do I seem angry?" Perriweather said.

"Say, you're really a good sport," Gloria said. "We'll start right up there."

"I'll be expecting you."

"Mr. Perriweather, you won't be sorry. The new plan will get rid of all your problems."

"Yes, it will," Perriweather said.

"You haven't even heard it yet."

"I'm sure it will. You and Nathan, I know, will get rid of all my problems," Perriweather said as he hung up.

Gloria Muswasser said to Nathan, "He's a little on the weird side, but he's okay. He wants us to come up to Massachusetts and tell him about the new plan. He wants us to solve all his problems."

"Bottom line. Really bottom line," Nathan said with authority.

13

The Muswassers arrived six hours late. First, they had gotten lost and wound up in Pennsylvania instead of Massachusetts. Then they had seen a theater playing their all-time favorite movie, *The China Syndrome*, so they stopped to see it for the twenty-seventh time.

When Perriweather met them at the door of his home, they offered him a flurry of secret handshakes. He politely refused them all so they shook each other's hands.

Perriweather escorted them into a sparsely furnished room in a far wing of the mansion.

"Wait till you hear our idea, Wally boy," said Gloria expansively.

"I'm sure it will be wonderful."

"We're sorry about the TNT and the atomic bomb. They just didn't work and we feel bad about it," Nathan said.

"You mustn't feel bad. After all, look at all the chimpanzees you helped destroy by getting that package delivered to Uwenda," Perriweather said sarcastically.

"Well, not as good as delegates directly," Gloria said. "But at least the chimps killed some of the delegates. That was good."

"It certainly was," Perriweather said agreeably. "So good that I thought you ought to be rewarded."

"That's real nice, Wally," Gloria said.

"Would you two care for a glass of sherry?" Perriweather asked.

"Got any weed?" Nathan said before his wife elbowed him in the ribs.

"Sherry'd be fine," Gloria said.

Perriweather nodded. "Good. I'll be right back. Wait here for me and then I'll show you how you're going to fit into our great new plan of attack." He closed the door to the room behind him as he went out.

Gloria and Nathan roamed around the room with its two metal chairs and small plastic Parsons table.

"Look at this," Nathan said. He picked up a framed object from the table and handed it to Gloria. It was a collection of little human-shaped dolls speared through their torsos with pins, their arms and legs splayed wide like the appendages of insects in a display cage.

"He's buggy," Nathan whispered. "Don't tell me."

"He's into bugs," Gloria said.

"I thought the Species Liberation Alliance meant animals," Nathan said. "Like puppies and things. Harp seals. Endangered species. Who the hell ever endangered a bug species?"

"That's because you're narrow-minded," Gloria said. "Bugs are animals. They sure aren't vegetable or mineral. And since Perriweather's been putting up all the money for the SLA, I guess he ought to have a say in what we try to liberate."

"Yeah, but bugs aren't cute," Nathan said as he put the display case back on the table. "Ever try to snuggle up to a mosquito?"

"That's your bourgeois unliberated upbringing," Gloria said. "You have to learn to accept bugs as your equals."

The library door opened a crack and a tiny buzzing creature flew in. The door closed sharply behind it, and Gloria heard a sound like two heavy bolts sliding into place inside the door.

"What's that?" Nathan said.

"It's a fly," Gloria said.

"It's got red wings."

"Maybe it's a pet. Maybe it wants to be friends." The fly was circling around Nathan's head. "Go ahead, Nathan. Hold out your hand to it."

"It wants to crap on my hand," Nathan said.

"Nathan," Gloria said menacingly.

"Ah, I never met a fly that wanted to shake hands before," Nathan said.

"That was in the old days. Our whole way of thinking about our insect friends has to change," Gloria said.

"All right, all right," Nathan said.

"Go ahead. Give the fly your hand."

"What if he bites it?"

"Stupid. Little flies don't bite."

"Some of them do," Nathan said.

"What of it? Maybe he needs the nourishment. You wouldn't want it to starve, would you? For lack of a little blood when you've got so much of it?"

"I guess not," Nathan said miserably and held out his arm.

"That's better," Gloria said. "Come on, little fly. We'll call him Red. Come on, Red. Come say hello to Gloria and Daddy Nathan."

The fly landed in the crook of Nathan's elbow.

From outside the door to the room, Waldron Perriweather III heard a shriek, then a growl. And then another shriek as Gloria too was bitten.

He slid shut yet a third steel bolt in the door, patted the door, and a thin smile creased his face.

* * *

Dr. Dexter Morley was frantic when he burst into Perriweather's study.

"They're gone. Both of them. I just went to the bathroom for a moment and when I came back they were gone."

"I have the flies," Perriweather said.

"Oh. Thank heavens. I was so worried. Where are they?"

"I told you I'd take care of them." Perriweather's eyes were like ice.

"Yes, sir," Morley said. "But you've got to be really careful with them. The're very dangerous."

Although the ice-blue eyes were still frozen, Perriweather's lips formed a tight smile. "You've achieved quite a milestone, Doctor," he said.

Morley fidgeted. Praise seemed not to belong on Perriweather's lips. He nodded because he did not know what else to do.

"You asked me, Doctor, how I had produced the other changes in that fly. The ability to bite and its effect on creatures that it did bite."

"Yes. I am really interested in that."

"The truth is, Doctor . . ." Perriweather rose to his feet. "I've taken the liberty of inviting a few friends over to help us celebrate. I didn't think you'd mind."

"Of course not."

"They're waiting for us. Why don't we walk over there?" Perriweather said. He clapped a big hand on Dr. Morley's shoulder and steered the scientist toward the door. As they walked, he continued talking.

"Actually, I had another scientist working earlier for me," Perriweather said. "Those two breakthroughs were his. But he could never come up with the big breakthrough. That honor was reserved for you."

"Thank you. That's very kind. Who was the other scientist?" Morley asked.

Perriweather paused with Morley outside a door. Quietly he began to slide back the bolts in the door.

"Yes, it was a great achievement," Perriweather said. "You've made the new species unkillable and that should put your name in the honor rolls of science for all time. You made only one little mistake."

"Oh, what was that?"

"You said the flies should be ready to breed in a few weeks?"

"Yes."

"They already have and we've got pretty little maggots already growing on that piece of meat."

"Oh my God. They've got to be destroyed. If one gets out . . . they've got to be destroyed."

"Wrong again, Dr. Morley. *You've* got to be destroyed."

He pulled the door open, pushed the scientist inside, and slammed the door shut, pushing the bolts back in place.

There were growls, no longer recognizable as the voices of Gloria and Nathan Muswasser. Then there was a scream, a thump and the sickening sound of flesh being torn from bone.

Perriweather knew the sound. He pressed his ear to the door and reveled in it. As a child, he had once torn the flesh from a cat in the gardener's toolshed. He had found some carpenter's tools, a vise and a clamp, and had used them to dismember the animal. The cat had sounded like that too. And Perriweather had felt the same satisfaction then.

He'd caught the cat playing with a spiderweb. The cat had trapped the spider and had been playing with it as if it were some kind of toy. He had taught the cat a lesson. And then, when the gardener had caught him with the bloody cat in his hands, he had taught the gardener a lesson too.

The gardener had tried to untangle the dead cat from the clamps and while he was working and muttering that young Waldron was going to learn the difference between right and wrong, by God, the boy had calmly and silently moved a stool behind the old man, climbed on it, lifted a brick over his head and smashed it into the spotted, white-haired skull. Then he had set fire to the shed and that was the end of the gardener. Along with all his insecticides and poisons.

It was in those earlier memories that the SLA had taken form. Of course, Waldron Perriweather couldn't care less about most animals. They were coarse, hygiene-obsessed things that cared as little for insects as human beings did. But when he had first tried recruiting people for the Insect Liberation Front, no one had seemed particularly interested. Human beings were self-centered creatures who wanted to believe that they were the superior species of earth. Most of them didn't even know that they were outnumbered by insects more than a million to one. As far as most ignorant humans were concerned, insects were objects to be swatted without a thought. Little boys tore the wings off flies for sport. Housewives regularly sprayed their kitchens with fly poisons. They let out plastic containers that emitted toxic fumes just to avoid sharing their space with flies. The injustice of it was too great to be borne.

But he couldn't interest anyone in the Insect Liberation Front, so quietly, using a lot of other people as the up-front leaders, he had begun the Species Liberation Alliance. He put up the money and directed it. In the early days, the public members took the credit. Now, as the group had become more violent in its methods, the public members took the blame. All

Waldron Perriweather got was the satisfaction of a job well done.

But now the battle was almost over. He had his invincible weapon. One of them was alive in the Plexiglas cube in his office, and another twelve were little maggots, gorging themselves on rancid beef. In another day or two, they would be red-winged beauties too. Ready to take their revenge on the earth.

Upstairs, in the dusty quiet room housing the jeweled miniature casket, Perriweather spoke softly to the withered black insect.

"It has begun, Mother," he said. "I told you that your death would be avenged. The punishment is coming for all those who could so casually kill our kind as if we were of no importance. They will see our importance, Mother. The new red-winged fly will be our avenging angel."

He thought for a moment. "There are two obstacles yet to deal with, Mother. The two new scientists at the IHAEO laboratory. From what I hear, they claim to be even further advanced than Dr. Ravits was. And they were responsible for the mass murder in Uwenda, wiping out the Ung beetle."

A tear rolled down his cheek as he thought of the horrible numbers of insects killed. "They're monsters, Mother. But don't worry. Their time is coming. This Dr. Remo and this Dr. Chiun will see no more sunrises."

14

Barry Schweid had finally simplified the steps necessary to get the information from the small attaché-case computer. Smith still did not understand how Schweid was able to use something he called cosmic energy for storage, but that didn't matter. It was enough that any bit of information that went into CURE's main computers at Folcroft and on St. Martin Island would instantly be transferred to the small hand-held attaché case. And now Smith no longer needed Schweid to access that information: he could get it himself.

Schweid had also worked out the erasure mechanisms for the main computer. He had already installed it on the St. Martin equipment and when Smith went back to Folcroft, he would do the same with the mainframe computers there. CURE's information would be safe from invasion. If anyone should ever enter the computer line, it would instantaneously erase itself.

It was absolute safety, absolutely foolproof, and Smith felt good.

Until he felt the click in the attaché case which meant that there was a telephone call for him.

When he opened the case, he saw a small green light lit. That meant the call was coming from his office in Rye, New York, and he was surprised.

The green light had never been lit before. Mrs. Mikulka, his secretary, was far too efficient to require any help from him during the time he spent away from the office.

Actually, it was Mrs. Mikulka who ran the day-to-day operations of the sanitarium, and her salary, if not her title, reflected it. She knew nothing about CURE and if her superior often seemed inordinately engrossed in some business that needed no one but himself to run it, she kept that opinion to herself. Actually, she believed that Smith had himself some kind of time-consuming hobby, like correspondence chess, and not a business that he organized and managed, because she felt that Harold Smith was one of those men who could not organize a button into a buttonhole unaided.

"Yes, Mrs. Mikulka," he said into the small portable telephone in the case.

It couldn't be anything bad, Smith thought. His security problems with the computers were solved; Remo had obviously found and disarmed the atomic weapon because there had been no explosion, and he had faith that Remo and Chiun would soon put an end to whoever was behind the attacks on the IHAEO labs. And Dr. Ravits' great scientific breakthrough was safe and now belonged to the world's scientific community. The day might come when the world would be free of destructive insects, and if that happened, CURE could take some of the quiet credit. Nothing bad could happen to Smith now.

"I'm sorry to bother you, Dr. Smith," Mrs. Mikulka said hesitantly. There was a catch in her voice. Her words trailed off into silence.

"Hello. Mrs. Mikulka, are you there?"

"Yes, sir," the woman said. "I don't know quite how to tell you this . . ."

"Go ahead, please," Smith said, but tried not to be snappish with the woman. "I'm expecting another call and I'd like to keep this conversation brief." The truth was, Smith was expecting no other call. He didn't like to tie up any telephone line. The more words, the more chance of someone overhearing them.

"Of course," sir," she said. "The offices have been broken into."

"The computers downstairs?" Smith said.

"No, they weren't touched. It was my desk."

"What in the desk?" Smith asked mildly, feeling a wave of relief flood his body. There was nothing of importance to CURE in her desk.

"Your telephone book, sir."

Telephone book? All the telephone numbers in the world had been programmed into the Folcroft computers years before.

"The old book," she continued. "The address book you gave me. It was before you built your computers. You had me type all your numbers into a directory. I think it was in 1968."

He remembered. It was taking a risk back then, having eyes other than his own see the material he was assembling to put into the computers. For that reason, he had never hired a permanent secretary, using instead an endless series of temporary typists to handle the overwhelming paperwork.

The typists were dull things as a rule, slow and sometimes too inquisitive about reports that obviously had nothing to do with the administration of a nursing home for the elderly. Only Mrs. Mikulka, on the days she worked for Smith, met his requirements. She was fast, well-organized and totally accurate, and most important, asked no questions about the work.

Eventually, after the computers were installed, Smith took her on permanently, knowing that the sanitarium business at Folcroft would run smoothly and unobtrusively under her keen and discreet eye.

But the telephone book was different. It contained a list of numbers, all coded but decipherable, of every contact CURE had used up until 1968. It contained the name of the man who had first recruited Remo, all the upper-echelon Pentagon personnel, leaders of foreign countries, large-scale crime bosses and the like.

The information the book contained was of secondary importance. Most of the cast of characters had changed in the intervening years. The danger of the book lay in the fact of its very existence and that it could lead an intelligent observer to wonder who would compile such a list of numbers and possibly bring him to the realization that America had a super-secret agency working outside the law.

It meant exposure for CURE and once it was exposed, CURE was finished.

"You're sure the book is missing?" Smith asked. "Maybe you destroyed it years ago?"

"I'm sure, sir. I didn't trust the computers at the time. I thought they might do something wrong and erase everything, so when I saw the old telephone book on your desk, I wanted to please you so I picked it up and put it in my desk drawer and it was in the back of the drawer for seventeen years."

"How do you know it was stolen?" Smith asked.

"I . . ." She faltered. "I think I know who took it, Dr. Smith."

"Yes?"

"My son."

Smith struggled to keep his voice calm. "What makes you say that?"

"It was my fault, Dr. Smith," she sobbed. "He's a good boy, really. It's just that he always gets into trouble."

"Please tell me only the facts," Smith said calmly. "It's important. What is your son's name?"

"Keenan, after my husband. But it was my fault. I told him."

"Told him what?"

Mrs. Mikulka sounded nearly hysterical over the telephone. "Keenan came home the other night. It's been so long since we've seen him. He was traveling so much, and then there was some business with a robbery and he spent some time in prison. Not a maximum-security prison, mind . . ."

Smith began to form a mental picture of the man who was his secretary's offspring: a lonely, unlikable young felon who always looked for the easy way out. A mugger, thief, a check forger, a petty criminal.

Smith wanted to chastise himself for hiring Mrs. Mikulka without checking into the backgrounds of all her family members. Her own background was impeccable; nothing about her had ever been out of place.

"Did you talk to him about me?" Smith asked.

"It was just talk, Dr. Smith," she pleaded. "Keenan was home and for once he didn't just ask for money. I made him his favorite dinner and afterward we sat and talked, just Keenan and me, like the old days before he left home. It was just talk."

"Just talk about what?" he asked.

He heard her weeping.

"I'm so ashamed. I've never said a word about you before . . ."

"Please go on, Mrs. Milkulka," Smith said.

"I just mentioned casually that you seemed so awfully busy for a man without much to do. I mean . . ."

"I understand. What else?"

"Just that you were always at Folcroft from sunrise until midnight and the only people you ever saw were the young man with the thick wrists and the old Chinese man. Keenan said it sounded like you were covering something up, and I . . . well, I mentioned the old phone book, I don't know why it popped in my head, and the names in it that didn't make any sense like ELYODDE. I remember that was one of them. And Keenan asked me if I still had the book and at first I said I didn't because it was so long ago but then I remembered that it was probably still in my desk."

"I see," said Smith. He felt the color drain from his face.

"Keenan asked me to get the book for him," Mrs. Mikulka said.

"Did you?"

"Of course not," she said indignantly. "I told him I was going to burn it in the morning, now that I'd remembered about it. Especially since you never seemed to need it, not once in all those seventeen years. I don't know what you spend your time on, Dr. Smith, but I know it's nobody's business but yours. Not mine and not Keenan's."

"Yes," Smith said vaguely.

"But then this morning when I woke up, Keenan was gone with all his things. He wasn't supposed to leave until next week. That's what his ticket said. And then when I got to the office, there was this mess . . ."

"Wait a minute, Mrs. Mikulka. His ticket to where?"

"Puerto Rico. You see, Keenan just came into some money. I didn't ask him where he got it."

"San Juan? Is that where he's going? Do you know exactly where he's staying?"

The line was silent for a long moment. Then the woman said, "He said he was staying in another city. With a funny name. He said he had a friend there, someone he'd spent time in prison with. Crystal Ball, that's it."

"Cristobal? San Cristobal?"

"Yes, I think so."

"What's the name of the friend?"

"That I'm sure of," she said. "Salmon."

"Er . . . salmon?"

"Like the fish. Except Keenan pronounced it sal-*moan.*" Mrs. Mikulka paused and then blurted out a question: "Would you like me to leave immediately, Dr. Smith? Or should I finish off the work I've got first?"

Smith's mind was already hundreds of miles away, already planning an action in the mountain village of San Cristobal in central Puerto Rico.

"Dr. Smith?" she said.

"I beg your pardon," he said.

"My resignation. I know it's necessary and if I've been party to some kind of a crime, I'm willing to take the consequences for that," she said unemotionally. "I just wanted you know I didn't do it on purpose."

"Don't resign," Smith said. "Don't even think of that now. We will discuss all that some other time, Mrs. Mikulka."

He hung up and looked at Barry Schweid, who was sitting across the room, trying to get a suntan through a tightly closed window.

"Need any help, Harold?" Schweid said.

"No. I want to use this computer to trace an airline ticket."

"Go ahead. I showed you how."

Within a few seconds, Smith had confirmed that one Keenan Mikulka had booked passage on a commercial airline to San Juan. The ticket had been used.

Smith closed the attaché case and stood up.

"Barry, I'm going to have to go away for a day or so.'

"I'm going to be by myself here?"

"Yes. This is a nice apartment and there's food in the refrigerator."

"What should I do if the telephone rings?" Schweid asked.

"Answer it, Barry," said Smith.

"If it's for you, Harold?"

"Take a message, Barry."

Smith's face was grim. "I have to go now, Barry."

"Take me with you," Barry said.

Smith shook his head. "I can't. Not this time."

He walked out the door. Behind him, Barry Schweid whimpered, "Please," and clutched his blue blanket.

15

Smith drove carefully over the rutted dirt road leading to San Cristobal, his left hand resting lightly on an attaché case that was an exact duplicate of the one which contained CURE's computers.

Smith had locked the computer case in one of the luggage lockers at San Juan Airport. Both cases had passed through security without a glance. Smith had produced a card bearing a false name and that false name had been greeted with the deference due a visiting king, even though Smith had flown in from St. Martin, which was technically a foreign country. None of the officials recognized the face of the middle-aged man in the three-piece suit but their orders were to extend him every courtesy.

Even a car was waiting, a gleaming gray Mercedes, but Smith had exchanged it for a nondescript Ford.

He turned down the offer of a driver from airport officials. Smith had lived a lifetime of secrecy and did not like ostentation. He was intentionally forgettable-looking, and his manner was bland and innocuous. It was the way men like Smith were trained to look and to live.

That very look of harmlessness was what often kept Smith's sort alive. It had kept him alive throughout the

Second World War and during Korea with the CIA
and through the beginning of CURE.

Now that Remo was the agency's enforcement arm,
Smith no longer had to stay in the kind of physical
condition his profession had once required, but the
secretive cast of mind remained. It was an ingrained
part of him, as necessary as his steel-rimmed
eyeglasses.

He entered San Cristobal through a back road and
parked on a dusty side street. The street was hot in the
blistering afternoon and nearly lifeless. A fat
housewife shuffled a brood of children into a store
where flies peered out through dirty glass. A lame dun-
colored dog limped into an alleyway looking for a
scrap of garbage.

The only sounds of life came from a bar a hundred
feet from where Smith had parked. There, the voices
made the kind of hollow noises of men with too much
time and too little money. Smith walked down the
block, into the bar, and stood at the dirty metal
counter.

"*Si, señor?*" the bartender asked.

"*Cerveza, por favor,*" said Smith. When the beer
came, Smith asked in broken Spanish if the bartender
knew a man named Salmon.

The man furrowed his brow in concentration and
Smith repeated, "Sal-*moan,*" accenting the second
syllable.

To his surprise, the bartender threw the dirty bar
rag in front of Smith and turned his back on him. The
other men in the bar were silent for a moment, then
burst into raucous laughter.

"*Señor,*" a man with a creased red face said, as he
walked up to Smith. "It is clear you do not understand. Salmon is a . . . how do you call it, nickname. It
means a fool, or a stupid lazy fellow. You see?" He

raised his eyebrows inquiringly, then translated what he had just said for the other six men in the tavern.

"*Es Rafael, si,*" one of them shouted with a laugh. The bartender shook his fist at him.

"You have hurt Rafael's feelings," the red-faced man told Smith.

"Oh, I'm sorry," Smith said mildly. He began to apologize as best he could to the barman, but as he began to speak, a barrel-chested man who had been sitting at at table at the side of the room stood up. His eyes met Smith's and then he walked curtly toward the open entrance out into the street.

Smith took a sip of his beer, figured that his beer was ninety cents, debated about waiting for his change, then left a full dollar on the bar. The ten-cent tip might assuage the bartender's hurt feelings, he thought.

The street outside was empty. Smith thought for a moment that the man's exit had meant nothing, but he dismissed the thought. Decades of spy work had made him aware of the meanings behind even simple gestures, and he had to trust his instincts. Without them, he had nothing else.

He saw it then, suspended on an ironwork pole near the top of a run-down three-story building down the block. A sign. There were no words on it, only the drawing of a fish. A salmon?

He saw an open door at ground level and walked into a room devoid of furniture but cluttered with boxes and crates. A few bits of paper were strewn on the floor. In the corners stood rows of empty beer bottles. A shabby middle-aged woman with a face frozen into a permanent scowl waddled toward him down a corridor from the back of the apartment.

"*Si?*" she demanded with the air of one whose privacy had been violated.

"I'm looking for a man," he tried to explain in Spanish. "An American—"

"No men," she snapped in passable English. "Women only. You want?"

"No. I don't want a woman."

"Then go."

"I am looking for a man."

"Ten dollars."

"I . . ."

"Ten dollars," the woman repeated.

Smith handed her a bill reluctantly, then followed the woman to a filthy kitchen in the back of the store.

"I just want to talk," Smith said.

"Follow me," the woman said. She led Smith up a rickety flight of stairs to the top landing. In the dim, roach-swarming corridor, she knocked brusquely on a door, then pushed it open. "You talk in here," she said, pushed Smith inside, and closed the door behind him.

Smith's eyes took a moment to adjust to the darkness of the room. When they did, they rested on a solitary figure, a young woman with a tumble of black curls falling over her shoulders. She was sitting cross-legged on a rumpled corner of the bed, wearing shorts and a tight cotton shirt whose three buttons barely contained the ample flesh of her bosom.

Smith cleared his throat. "That's not necessary, Miss," he said, annoyed that his voice was barely audible. "Do you speak English? *Habla usted ingles?*"

The girl untangled her long legs from beneath her and rose. Her shorts stretched across her hips tantalizingly. She walked toward him, wordlessly, the hint of a smile playing on her lips.

Smith didn't know what gave her away. A glance of her eyes, perhaps, or a tension in her body as she snaked toward him. He did not know the reason but he was ready when he heard the first sound of the ambush.

Smith was no longer a young man and his reflexes were slow compared with what they had been during his days as an active agent. But no one with his background ever lost the razor-sharp sting of fear or forgot what to do when he felt it. Crouching and whirling about abruptly, he connected an elbow with someone's midsection. The assailant staggered backward in the darkened room, air whooshing from his lungs.

It gave Smith enough time to draw his automatic from the shoulder holster. He followed the man downward and planted one foot on the man's neck while he aimed the gun directly at the man's face.

"You get back on the bed," Smith growled over his shoulder at the young woman. He heard her soft footsteps move away, and then the squeak of the bed springs.

Smith recognized the man's face. It was the man who had led him from the bar.

"Sal-moan," Smith said. It was not a question.

The man grunted and Smith dug the heel of his shoe into the flesh of the man's neck.

"Are you Salmon?" Smith said. He pressed his foot down harder.

With an effort, the Puerto Rican nodded, his eyes bulging.

"Why did you set me up?" Smith ground his heel in harder. The barrel-chested man gestured helplessly and Smith lightened the pressure enough to allow the man to speak.

"Not my idea," the man gasped. "It's not me you want."

"I know who I want. Why did he send you to me?"

"The book—"

"Has he got it?"

Salmon nodded.

"I'm going to pay for it," Smith said.

The Puerto Rican's eyes widened.

"You don't think I will, because I have a gun?" Smith said. "I don't want to use the gun and I don't want you two to follow me. I want that book and I'll pay for it. You understand?"

The man nodded.

Keeping the barrel of the gun flush against Salmon's head, Smith stepped back. "Get up," he said.

The man shambled to his feet, watching Smith carefully as the American picked up his leather attache case.

"I want to see Keenan Mikulka," Smith said.

Salmon drove Smith's car at gunpoint through the gently rolling tropical hills. The macadam roads became gravel, then dirt, then little more than trails with grassy strips between two rows of tire-worn earth. He stopped the car at the foot of a hill dense with scrub bush and giant tropical ferns.

"Can't go no further," the Puerto Rican said. "Got to walk now."

Smith leveled the gun at his face. "You first," he said.

They trekked up the overgrown hill, following a snaking foot trail. Halfway up the slope, Smith spotted a roof of corrugated tin shining in the red light of the lowering sun.

Salmon pointed. "He's in there," he said. "He's got a gun too."

His eyes never leaving Salmon's, Smith shouted: "Mikulka. Keenan Mikulka."

Silence.

"My name is Smith. I've got your friend. We're alone. Come down here. I want to talk."

After a moment, Smith heard the rustling of leaves near the shack, then a voice calling back:

"What do you want to talk about?"

"Business. I'll buy the telephone book from you."

"Who says I even know what you're talking about?"

Smith poked Salmon with the gun. "It's okay. He knows," the Puerto Rican yelled. "He's got money."

"How much?" the voice answered.

"We'll talk when I see you," Smith called out.

Footsteps sounded through the undergrowth. Finally a young man stepped into the clearing, across from Smith and Salmon.

Mikulka appeared to be in his late twenties with the seedy look of a man who had given up hoping or dreaming. An Army-regulation Colt was in his right hand, its barrel aimed directly at Smith.

"Suppose you put down that itty-bitty gun of yours," Mikulka said, smiling crookedly.

"It won't take a very big bullet to blow out your friend's brains," Smith said. The Puerto Rican was sweating profusely. "Let's go up to where you're staying. I want to deal."

"Suppose I don't?" Mikulka said.

Smith shrugged, a small economical gesture. "I've got the money," he said. "And more than one bullet."

The young man snorted derisively, but started to back up the hill.

Smith pushed Salmon forward, so that the Puerto Rican was sandwiched between the two guns.

The tin-roofed shack was sweltering and dark. Inside were a rumpled cot, a table and a small kerosene cookstove.

"Where's the money?" Mikulka demanded.

Smith tossed the attache case onto the dirty table, then snapped it open with one hand. The interior of the case was lined, corner to corner and as deep as the case, with United States currency. Old bills in stacks, encircled by rubber bands.

"How much is there?" Mikulka's voice betrayed his astonishment.

"A hundred thousand in unmarked twenties," Smith said.

"*Dios,*" Salmon breathed softly.

Smith placed his weapon on the table. Warily, Mikulka did the same.

"What's the deal?" the young man asked.

"I should think that's obvious," Smith said with some distaste. "You get the money and I get back the book you stole from me."

Mikulka chewed his lip. "Suppose I got other takers?" he taunted. "That ain't no list of call-Florrie-for-a-good-time. I think maybe some foreign countries might be willing to put up more than a hundred grand to find out just what you do all alone in that big office by yourself."

Salmon started to speak but Mikulka silenced him with a violent gesture.

"You haven't had time to make any contacts," Smith said evenly. "You probably haven't even broken the code and when you do, what'll you find? Seventeen-year-old phone numbers."

"I think I've got as much time as I want," Mikulka said. He lit a cigarette, holding it between his teeth.

"You're wrong, Mikulka. The information in that book is old material. No government will want it. It's old material."

"Then why do you want it so bad?" Salmon broke in.

"Sentimental value," Smith said. He turned back to

Mikulka. "At any rate, no foreign agent is going to pay you and let it go at that. You're in over your head, son."

"You don't know what you're talking about," Mikulka snapped.

"Sorry, but I do," Smith said. "First thing I know is that you're a cheap, unimportant nobody with a police record."

"Hey, wait a minute—"

Smith waved him down. "No intelligence service in the world is going to let you live for five minutes after they buy that document from you. If they *did* buy it. Don't you understand? You'll be killed. That's a guarantee."

The cigarette dangled nonchalantly from Mikulka's lips but his Adam's apple wobbled. He was frightened.

Good, Smith thought. The young man didn't know anything. It apparently had never occurred to him that the United States government would be as interested in the phone book as any foreign government. He had just stolen without thinking. But Smith had told him one great truth. No agent worth anything would let Mikulka or Salmon live for five minutes after getting the coded address book.

"Decision time," Smith said. "Will you take the money or not? I've got a plane to catch."

Mikulka hesitated, then motioned for Salmon to come closer. They exchanged whispers with their gazes riveted on Smith.

The CURE director did not have to hear them to know what was being said. They would sell him the book, take the money, then kill him, and resell the document to another buyer. It was the way it was always done in movies and it was the logic of the thief, to take and to take again. Thieves always thought like thieves; trained agents didn't.

"Yes or no?" Smith snapped the attaché case shut. As he did, his thumb broke a small piece of black metal off the right-hand clasp.

Five minutes, he thought.

"Suppose we want more time?" Mikulka suggested, his eyes mocking.

"I'm afraid you're out of time."

Mikulka and Salmon exchanged glances. From beneath the cot, Mikulka picked up a battered black leather address book and tossed it to Smith. "When you're out of time, you're out of time," he said with a halfhearted attempt at a grin.

Smith gave a polite nod, then picked his gun up from the table. Mikulka also retrieved his Colt. Another standoff.

"I think I ought to count that money," Mikulka said. "A hundred thousand, you said?"

"Right. Count it," Smith said. "I'm going to wait outside. With the book."

Four minutes.

He tucked the book into his jacket pocket and backed out of the shack. They were cowards, he knew, and would wait for him to turn his back. And he was counting on their trying to hide behind the walls of the shack while they picked him off.

As he moved outside, he saw the two men's eyes following him. Their faces wore the self-satisfied expressions of muggers cornering an old lady on an empty street.

Mikulka sat behind the table, opened the case and began to riffle through the money.

Smith backed away, twenty yards from the shack, standing there, looking at the rickety building.

Thirty seconds. He began to count down.

He heard movement from inside.

Fifteen seconds.

Fourteen. Thirteen. Twelve . . .

"It's all here," Mikulka called out.

"Good. Good-bye, then," Smith yelled.

Three seconds.

He turned his back, offering himself as a target. Then he threw himself on the ground a split second before the report of the gun sounded through the woods. He half-rolled toward the cover of a termite-eaten log.

And then there was another sound.

The explosion tore the roof off the shack, sending ribbons of metal raining over the forest in a light show of orange sparks. A wall of dirt and rotted vegetation shot upward in a circle, then plummeted down. Smith covered his head. A rock fell painfully onto his thigh but he did not move. Overhead, a thousand tropical birds screeched as a stand of bamboos toppled and crashed like toothpicks.

And then it was silent.

Smith dusted himself off and walked back to the ruins of the shack. Mikulka lay faceup in the debris. His features were unrecognizable. He had no eyes and his hands seemed to have been shredded by the blast. He must have been holding the case of money even as he was firing at Smith. Salmon's body was ripped into three fat parts.

In the dust and smoke, a piece of paper drifted. Smith caught it. It was part of a counterfeit twenty-dollar bill, one of five thousand identical bills Smith had carried in the exploding suitcase.

Smith felt the texture of the bill. It was a good copy.

Nearby, several small fires smoldered. He kicked one to life and when the flames were high enough, he took the address book from his pocket and threw it into the blaze. He waited until there was nothing left of the book except white ashes.

Then he stomped on the ashes and left.

Back in San Juan, he stopped at the Western Union office and sent a telegram to Mrs. Eileen Mikulka, care of Folcroft Sanitarium, Rye, New York:

DEAR MOTHER SORRY I CAUSED YOU SUCH GRIEF STOP AM SHIPPING OUT TODAY ON MERCHANT SHIP BOUND FOR SOUTH PACIFIC STOP NOT COMING BACK STOP I LOVE YOU STOP KEENAN.

Thirty words exactly. Smith thought about things like that.

16

Waldron Perriweather III strode easily into the office of Dara Worthington at IHAEO labs and handed the woman his card.

"I'm here to see Dr. Remo and Dr. Chiun," he said.

"I'm sorry, Mr. Periwinkle, but they are not available right now," Dara said, handing him his card back.

"It's Perriweather, not Periwinkle, you egg-layer," he said acidly. "Surely you've heard of me."

"What did you call me?"

"I called you an egg-layer."

"I know who you are," Dara said suddenly. "You're the lunatic who's always making excuses for violence."

"And you belong in a nest," Perriweather said. "Get those two scientists out here."

"You are the crudest—"

"In a nest with orange peels and coffee grounds on the bottom. Get them, I said."

Dara pressed an intercom button that made her voice reverberate around the IHAEO complex.

"I think you are a matter for security, Mr. Perriweather. You understand? Security."

"I have no intention of discussing anything with a breeder. Bring on your scientists."

Inside the main lab, Remo heard Dara's voice.

"Security," he said. "I think that's us."

Chiun unfolded himself from a lotus position atop one of the tables.

"About time," he grumbled. "No wonder scientists are always being given prizes. They deserve medals for their ability to endure boredom."

"I think some of them do more than sit on tables," Remo said.

"If they were afflicted with ungrateful pupils the way I am, they would be under the tables, not on them," Chiun said.

"Why don't we go see what Dara wants?" Remo said.

"If you wish. But if the two of you start noisily coupling in her office, I do not know if I will be able to control myself."

"I'll keep a lid on it, Little Father."

"See that you do."

"Ah. Drs. Remo and Chiun," Perriweather said. He handed his card toward Remo, who ignored it. He shoved it into Chiun's hand. Chiun tore it up.

"What seems to be the trouble, Dara?" Remo asked.

"This one called me an egg-layer."

Chiun chuckled. "An egg-layer," he snorted. "What a wonderful term for the white female."

Dara threw her hands up over her head in exasperation and stormed from the office.

"I am Chiun," the Korean said to Perriweather, nodding slightly.

"And you must be Dr. Remo?" Perriweather said.

"Just Remo will do."

Perriweather thrust his hand forward toward Remo, who ignored it. In a quick glance, Perriweather appraised the young man with the thick wrists. He didn't look much like a scientist. He looked more like a security man, probably around to protect the old Oriental. He smiled involuntarily. The late Dr. Ravits could tell them a thing or two about the value of security men, he thought.

But no matter. It just made his work easier than he had expected it to be.

"I greatly admired your work on eradicating the Ung beetle from Uwenda," he said.

Remo had appraised Perriweather too. The man was too smooth, too well dressed and too polished to be a scientist. But his fingernails were dirty.

"You read about it in the papers?"

"Yes," Perriweather said. "You see, I have some interest in entomology myself. Have a very sophisticated lab in my home. You should see it."

"Why?" Remo said coldly.

"Because as the two foremost entomologists at IHAEO, your opinions on an experiment of mine would be really useful."

"His opinion would not be useful at all," Chiun said, glancing at Remo. "He does not even know the correct clothing to wear. How could you expect him to appreciate science?"

Perriweather looked at Chiun, then in confusion glanced at Remo.

"My opinion's as good as anybody else's," Remo said testily. "What kind of bug work do you do, Periwinkle?"

"Perriweather," the man corrected. "And please, say 'insect.' 'Bug' is a term . . ." He stopped and took a couple of deep breaths to calm himself. "They are not bugs. They are insects," he finally said. "And because of your magnificent work on the Ung beetle, I came to alert you to an even greater danger which I have managed to isolate in my laboratory."

"What is it?" Remo said.

"I'd rather show you," Perriweather said. He moved closer and Remo could smell the scent of decay and rotting food on the man's skin. "I know you people have had trouble here with terrorists. Well, since I have been working on this project, I've gotten threats. I expect an attack tonight on my laboratory."

"You've got to tell me something about what your work is about," Remo told Perriweather. "And please stand downwind."

"Don't tell him anything," Chiun told Perriweather. "He'll forget it in two minutes. He remembers nothing, that one."

There was something going on between these two that Perriweather did not understand, so he elected to talk only to Remo.

"There is a new strain of insect," Perriweather said. "If proliferates very quickly and if my guess is correct, it could rule the earth within weeks."

"Then why are you smiling?" Remo said.

"Just nerves, I guess," Perriweather said. He clasped a hand over his mouth. Remo noticed that the man's fingers were long and thin and sharply angled at the joints, like the legs of a spider.

"We'd better go see this thing," Remo said.

"I think it's important," Perriweather said. "I have a private plane waiting."

Remo took Chiun aside. "Talk to him for a few minutes. I want to call Smitty and check him out."

"Yes," Chiun said. As Remo walked to the door, Chiun called out, "You can tell the egg-layer to return to her post. Heh, heh. Egg-layer. Heh, heh."

Remo dialed the telephone and listened to the clicks as the call switched from Albany through Denver and through Toronto before a telephone finally rang on the island of St. Martin in the Caribbean.

"Hello?" a quavering voice said.

Remo paused before answering. "Who is this?" he said suspiciously.

"It's Barry," the voice whimpered. "I suppose you're calling for Dr. Smith?"

"Maybe," Remo said cautiously.

"I'll have to take a message. He's not here. I wish he was. I really miss him."

"Barry who? Who are you?" Remo asked.

"Barry Schweid. I'm Dr. Smith's best friend. His very best friend. You're the one called Remo, aren't you? What can I do for you?"

"When is Smitty coming in?"

"I don't know. I wish he was here right now. I don't like talking on the telephone," Barry Schweid said.

"Give him a message for me, will you?" Remo said.

"Go ahead. I'll write it down."

"Tell him I want to know about a man named Perriweather. Waldron Perriweather the Third."

"Does that begin with a P?" Barry asked.

Remo hung up.

In the mansion, Perriweather led them past the gleaming white laboratory toward a dark corridor.

"Don't you want us to see the lab?" Remo asked.

"In a moment. There are a few things I'd like to show you first. There's a room down here. Just follow me."

"Something doesn't smell right here," Chiun said in Korean as they followed a few paces behind Perriweather down the dusty carpeted hall.

"It could be his fingernails," Remo responded in Korean. "Did you see them?"

"Yet his clothes are immaculate."

"But what was that stuff about Dara being an egg-layer?" Remo asked.

"Oh, that," Chiun said in dismissal.

"Yes, that."

"When one is speaking of white women, all is fair," Chiun said.

"I'll ignore that," Remo said.

"He became incensed when you used the word 'bug,' " Chiun said.

"Strange for somebody who works with them all the time. Probably keeps them in his fingernails as pets."

"Silence," Chiun hissed in Korean.

"What?"

"There are sounds coming from the room at the end of the hall."

Remo pitched his hearing low. The old man was right. Behind the thick door at the end of the corridor something was breathing. Something huge from the sound of it. As they stepped closer, the breathing grew louder.

"Someone snoring, maybe," Remo said in Korean. "From the looks of this place, sleeping might be the most fun thing to do."

Chiun was not smiling.

"What's in there, Chiun?" Remo asked. "What kind of animal?"

"Two things," Chiun said.

The noise grew louder. Air was hissing out of lungs that sounded as if they were made of concrete. As they neared the doorway, they could smell something vile from inside the door. The air became foul and cold.

"Control your breathing," Chiun snapped in Korean.

The stench curled around them like smoke.

Perriweather stepped back from the doorway.

"What's in there?" Remo said.

"The things I want you to see," Perriweather said.

"Wait here for me. I've got to get something from the office."

"We'll wait," Remo said as Perriweather strode off.

To Chiun, Remo said, "Whatever is in there knows we are coming."

"And doesn't like the idea," Chiun said. The noises from inside the room stopped for a moment, then exploded startlingly, before stopping abruptly.

Suddenly, behind them, a steel panel dropped, sealing off the corridor. At that moment, the heavy door ahead of them swung open.

Chiun looked at the heavy steel-plate panel.

"Forward or back?" Remo said.

"I suppose we should see the surprise this lunatic has prepared for us," Chiun said.

The two men walked into the room. Two people, a man and a woman, were standing quietly inside, near the far wall. Their faces wore small smiles. Their hands were folded ceremoniously in front of them.

"Hello," said Remo. He turned to Chiun. "What do you make of this?"

"The animal sounds came from this room," Chiun said.

Gloria Muswasser smiled and she and Nathan moved away from each other. Between them, on the floor, was a puddle of blood in which floated a broken human skull. Gloria moved slowly toward Remo and Chiun.

"The wallpaper is red," Remo said, noticing it for the first time.

"It is not paper. It is blood," Chiun said.

Gloria opened her mouth. A vapor of foul-smelling gas belched from her like smoke from a chimney, along with a deep growl so loud and low it seemed to shake the walls. Her eyes glinted inhumanly.

"You ought to take something for that gas," Remo said. He casually extended a hand toward Gloria, but with one lightning-fast motion she swatted him across the room like a Ping-Pong ball. Instinctively Remo curled himself up and struck the wall with both feet, bouncing off unhurt.

"What the . . . ?"

Nathan was coming at him, shrilling like a police-car whistle. His arms were outstretched, his fingers bloodied, his eyes glazed. From the corner of his vision, Remo could see the woman coming toward him too, her teeth bared like a rabid dog's in a vicious rictus of hatred.

"Take care of the man," Chiun said softly.

Remo saw the old man's arms move in a gentle teasing circle, then heard a piercing shriek as Gloria, wild-eyed, whirled in her tracks to attack the Korean.

And then Nathan was moving toward Remo, his head down oxlike, but moving as fast as a blink. As he circled Remo, swatting and lunging, his movements so quick they were hard to follow, Remo ducked the man's unfocused attacks as best he could.

One crashing thump landed on Remo's shoulder blades, knocking the wind out of him. As Remo tried to rise, Nathan jumped into the air, a full six feet high, then slammed feetfirst toward Remo.

"All right," Remo growled. "Enough of this." He spun out of the way a split second before Nathan landed. The force of the man's feet broke the floor-boards beneath the carpet and Nathan sank in, his head tossing around bewilderedly.

"Hole," said Remo, pointing to the cavity around Nathan's feet.

"Naaaaargh," Nathan roared.

"Close enough," Remo said. He brought both fists down on Nathan's shoulders and concentrated his power on the points of impact. The big man fell through the floor with a deafening roar, pulling the carpet through the opening with him.

Remo glanced up to see Gloria lunging, screaming, toward Chiun. The old Oriental stood stock-still, his arms folded in front of him. He nodded toward Remo, who waited a split second, then stuck out his foot. She lurched forward, bellowing.

"Upsy daisy," Remo said, grabbing her foot and tossing her into the air.

She somersaulted twice, then fell facefirst into the hole through which the carpet had disappeared. She landed with a thunk.

"Adequate," Chiun told Remo.

"They're not growling anymore," Remo said. "Maybe they got knocked out."

"Not growling, but there is something else. Do you hear it?"

Remo listened. There was a low buzzing, faint but incessant, coming from the basement. Together the two men moved toward the hole in the floor as a swarm of flies, solidly black in the brightly-lit room, poured through the hole.

"I think we should leave," Remo said.

"Without knowing what is down there?" Chiun asked, pointing toward the hole.

"You go see. I'll wait here for you."

"The Master of Sinanju does not go climbing into basements."

Remo groaned to himself, then slid through the opening, blocking his breathing passages against the onslaught of flies that thickly blackened the cellar. As more insects escaped through the opening above, Remo could begin to see through the miasma of flying black bodies.

The bodies of the two creatures who had attacked

them were lying in twisted positions on a heap of
carpeting so covered with flies that they resembled
lumps of chocolate more than human forms. Remo
swatted a few dozen flies from their faces. Their eyes
were wide open and beginning to glaze.

"They're dead," Remo shouted.

"So?"

"So what else do you want? There are about ten
million flies down here," Remo said.

"So tell me something I don't know."

Remo looked around. As his eyes adjusted to the
darkness, he could make out some other shapes, all of
them fuzzy and soft-looking from the carpet of flies
covering them. Stomping and waving his arms, he
cleared the insects from one of the shapes.

"Jesus," he said softly, as he saw the white bones
emerge. It was the skeleton of a full-grown cow, its
bones picked nearly clean. Only a few ragged pieces of
rotting meat remained on the bones.

There were other skeletons, a dog, several cats, and
something with horns that Remo thought must once
have been a goat.

He jumped back up through the opening.

"It's a graveyard," he said. "Dead animals." He
paused.

"More than a graveyard?" Chiun asked.

"Like a restaurant. A restaurant for flies," Remo
said. "Let's get out of here."

By the time they had ripped down the heavy steel
panel and searched the house, it was empty. Perriweather had gone.

In the laboratory, nothing seemed out of place except for one Plexiglas cube with some elaborate
apparatus attached to it. There was nothing inside but
a piece of rancid meat and some flyspecks.

"You think this might mean something?" Remo asked.

"It is hardly the job of the Master of Sinanju to examine bug droppings," Chiun said haughtily. "We will leave those details to Emperor Smith. White men enjoy dung. That is how they invented disco dancing and frozen food."

Remo forced open a locked drawer and found inside a sheaf of papers covered with mathematical equations and illegible notes.

"These are letters and things. Notes. They belonged to . . . let's see." He turned over one of the envelopes. "A Dexter Morley. There's a bunch of letters after his name."

"Letters?" Chiun asked.

"Yeah. Degree letters. Like Ph.D. I think he's a doctor, whoever he is."

"Yes, a doctor. A veterinarian, no doubt," said Chiun, looking with distaste at the sinks filled with toads and salamanders.

17

When Smith entered the apartment in St. Martin, Barry Schweid was huddled in a corner, away from the bright sun, his blue blanket draped over his shoulders.

He looked up as Smith came in and his forlorn face suddenly lit up with joy, as intense and as consuming as the firing of a flashbulb.

"You came back. You really came back," Barry shouted. He lifted his pudge to his feet.

"As I told you I would, Barry," Smith said. He was carrying the small attaché case, containing the CURE files, which he had reclaimed from the airport locker in San Juan, Puerto Rico.

As he set it on a coffee table, the latch on the handle popped open, and with a sigh, Smith opened the case and picked up the telephone.

"Yes?"

"This is your office, Dr. Smith."

"I know who you are, Mrs. Mikulka."

The woman's voice was cheerier than it had been the previous day. "I just wanted you to know that . . . I think the problem was discussed . . . I mean . . ."

"I'm sure you have everything under control, Mrs. Mikulka," Smith said.

"Oh, it wasn't me. It was all very mysterious and then I got this telegram and—"

"Mrs. Mikulka, I really have to be on about my business," Smith said. "Perhaps this conversation will wait."

"I understand, Dr. Smith. About my resignation . . ."

"You're not resigning," Smith said flatly.

"I thought you'd want me to," she said.

"I don't know where you got that idea," Smith said.

"Well, it . . . , uh, well . . ." she sputtered.

"Carry on, Mrs. Mikulka."

When he replaced the phone, Barry Schweid asked, "Can I get you some Kool-Aid, Harold?"

"No, Barry."

"Here. I already poured it." He handed Smith a glass of something vaguely green.

Smith took it. "It's not cold," he said.

"The ice melted. I poured it yesterday just after you left. I really missed you, Harold."

Smith cleared his throat.

"I tried to fill up my time, though. I collected rocks and worked on cosmic refractions that store all your files and talked to your friend Remo on the telephone."

"What?" Smith glared at the butterball little man. "Why didn't you tell me sooner? When did he call?"

"This morning. He said something about a man named Perriweather."

"What about him?" Smith said angrily.

"He didn't know. He wanted you to find out who he was." As Schweid spoke, he opened Smith's attaché case and began to speak aloud as he typed onto the keyboard:

"Waldron Perriweather the Third, Address . . ."

Smith went into the kitchen, poured out the Kool-

Aid and drew a glass of cold water from the faucet.

When he reentered the living room, Schweid handed him a long sheet of paper. Smith glanced at it, then nodded.

"Did I do good, Harold? Are you happy with me?"

"You did fine, Barry," Smith said. He called Remo at the IHAEO labs but was told they were out of town in Massachusetts.

Reading from Barry Schweid's computer printout, Smith dialed Perriweather's telephone number.

"Speak," came a familiar voice.

"Smith here. What's on your mind, Remo?"

"What's on my mind is that last night we had to get rid of an atomic bomb. And now we've got three bodies here and a goddamn bone zoo. You think you could cut short the island madness and come lend a hand?"

"Who are the three bodies?" Smith asked.

"Don't know."

"Who killed them?"

"We did. Well, two of them," Remo said. "Listen, Smitty, there's too much to explain over the phone. Speaking of which, who's the dork you have answering the phone? I didn't think anybody was allowed to answer your phone."

"That's usually correct," Smith said. "But these were extraordinary circumstances."

"What's that mean?"

"I was called away on business," Smith said.

"What'd you do, find a store that was giving bigger discounts on paper clips? Come on, Smitty, let's get on the ball. Things are cooking around here."

"I'd rather not stay on this open line too long," Smith said.

"All right, one thing more," Remo said. "A name. Dexter Morley. I think he's a professor or something."

"What about him?"

"He's the one we didn't kill."

"How did he die?"

"If he's the one I think, in a puddle."

"A puddle of what?"

"A puddle of himself. That's all that was left of him except for some papers we can't make out, scientific stuff. That is, if he's even the corpse. We don't know."

"I'll be back in a few hours," Smith said as he replaced the receiver.

Barry sat back down in the corner, wrapped the sliver of blanket around him like a silk scarf and stuck the end of it in his mouth and stared glassily, pouting ahead.

"Now, Barry, stop that," Smith said. He frowned to cover his embarrassment at seeing a grown man and the smartest man he'd ever met acting like an infant.

"You're the only friend Blankey and I ever had," the fat man whimpered, still staring straight ahead. "And now you're going away."

"Blankey has no feelings," Smith said. "It's an inanimate object. Blankey . . ." He stopped, annoyed with himself for referring to a blanket as if it were a person. "You've just go to learn to get along without me sometimes. After all, you got along before you met me, didn't you?"

"Wasn't the same," Barry sniffed.

Unable to deal with irrationality, Smith left the room to pack his things.

It was inexplicable, Smith thought as he placed his extra three-piece gray suit, identical to the one he was wearing, in a plastic garment bag that he had gotten free from a clothing store fifteen years earlier. He was the farthest thing from a father image that he could think of, and yet the computer genius had grabbed onto him as if he were Smith's little boy.

It was ridiculous. Even Smith's own natural daughter had never been dandled on his knee or told a bedtime story. His wife, Irma, always took care of those things, and like a sensible woman, Irma had understood that her husband was not the type of man one clung to for emotional comfort. Harold Smith did not believe in emotion.

He had spent his entire life looking for truth, and truth was not emotional. It was neither good nor bad, happy nor distressing. It was just true. If Smith was a cold man, it was because facts were cold. It didn't mean that he wasn't human. He just wasn't a slobbering fool. At least Irma had had the intelligence always to realize that.

Now why couldn't Barry Schweid understand that? If Smith wanted to play father in some misguided moment of maudlinism, he hardly would have picked an emotional cripple whose only solace in life was a ratty old blanket. It embarrassed Smith even to think of him. Fat, homely Barry Schweid with the gumption of a hamster.

What complicated it all was that the sniveling wreck possessed the brain of an Einstein, and genius had to be forgiven some shortcomings.

But not this. No, Smith decided. He would not take Barry Schweid back to the United States. He would not be manipulated by childish tears into living out the rest of his life with an overweight albatross wrapped around his neck, clutching onto a spittle-covered blanket. No.

He zipped up the plastic garment bag to the spot halfway where the zipper no longer worked, then taped the rest of it together with pieces of masking tape. He carried the bag out into the living room.

"I think we've come up with something," Barry said without turning around. He was kneeling on the floor near the coffee table and Smith's attache´ case. His blanket was on his shoulder.

"What do you mean?" Smith said.

"That name you wrote down. Dexter Morley. He's a prominent entomologist from the University of Toronto. In earlier years, he was an associate of Dr. Ravits, the one who was killed. He helped Ravits to isolate pheromones, the substances that attract animals to each other. Then two years ago, he disappeared."

"Interesting," Smith said blandly. It *was* interesting. Ravits had been killed by terrorists, and now Remo may have found the body of Dr. Dexter Morley, a former Ravits associate, also dead. And he had been killed in the home of Waldron Perriweather III, who was a well-known spokesman for animal groups. Was it possible that Perriweather was behind all the violence?

"I looked it up in the computer," Barry said. "Actually, I knew that part already. Most scientists know about Morley's disappearance a couple of years ago. But I found out something even more interesting."

"What's that?"

"Will you take me with you?" Barry said. He turned tearful eyes toward Smith.

"No, Barry," Smith said. "I will not."

"I just wanted to go with you."

"Quite impossible. Now will you give me that information or not? It will save me a few minutes' work."

"All right," Barry whined. "I learned about Dr. Morley when I was in school because I studied entomology. Some believed that Morley had made a scientific breakthrough on the pheromones and left because he did not want to share credit with Dr.

Ravits. Others thought that he had just had a breakdown and ran away."

"Well?" Smith said impatiently.

"Because the name came in in connection with Perriweather, I started to look at banks where Perriweather lives. And there's a Dexter Morley listed at the Beverly First Savings with a bank balance of two hundred and one thousand dollars."

Smith arched an eyebrow, and pleased by the man's reaction, Barry rushed along with his story.

"I'm sure it's him. I've cross indexed him a lot."

"So Morley might have been hired away from Ravits at a big salary increase?" Smith said.

"I couldn't find anything about an employer, though," Barry said. "All the deposits were made in cash."

"I presume because the employer didn't want anyone to know about it," Smith said.

"Morley must have lived with his employer too because there's no listing of him as homeowner, tenant or telephone user within a hundred-mile radius of Beverly."

"Interesting," Smith said.

"I could really be helpful," Barry wheedled. His brow creased.

"I don't know, Barry," Smith said.

"Just tell me what you need, Harold. I want to earn my way. You'll be glad you took me along. Really you will. I can install the device on your other computers to prevent break-in. I'm better at that than you are. And I can help with this Dexter Morley. I studied entomology for three years."

"Three years isn't very much study in a field like that, is it?" Smith asked.

Barry looked hurt. "In three years, I read every major work on the subject written in English. My reading in French and Japanese was extensive too. I had to read German and Chinese in translation."

"I see," Smith said.

"They were good translations though," Barry offered. "Give me a chance, Harold."

Barry rose from the table, biting his lip. The fingers clutching the piece of paper in his hand were white.

Barry might be helpful, Smith thought, in translating Dexter Morley's notes, if those were what Remo had. But what would Smith do with him after that? After the project was over and done with, and there was no more use for Barry Schweid, what would Smith do with him? There was an answer in the back of his mind, but he did not want to think about it. Not now.

"After I'm done, I'll take care of myself," Schweid said.

"It's only a work project," Smith said.

"For you, it's only a project."

Smith sighed. "All right," he said finally.

Barry's face broke into a large grin.

"But I won't be responsible for you before, during or after. Is that clear?"

"Like crystal," Barry Schweid said adoringly.

Smith ground his teeth together in frustration as he closed the attaché-case computer. Something told him he had just made a terrible mistake. Barry was too attached to him and now Smith was taking him into a real world, a world where people had the power to kill and were not reluctant to use that power. Would the slings and arrows of ordinary life destroy the fragile young man?

Smith closed his eyes for a moment to squeeze the thought away. There was nothing he could do about it. After all, he was not Barry Schweid's keeper.

But then, he thought, who was?

* * *

Remo and Chiun were still waiting when Smith arrived at the Perriweather mansion.

"I trust the police haven't been here yet," Smith said.

"Nobody alive to call them," Remo said. "Except us, and we don't like the police stomping around. Who's that?" He cocked his head toward the rotund little man who seemed to be trying to hide behind Smith.

Smith cleared his throat. "Errr, this is my associate, Barry Schweid."

"And Blankey," Barry said.

"And Blankey?" Remo said.

"And Blankey," Barry said, holding up the piece of blue material.

"Oh," Remo said. "Well, you and Blankey stay right there. We have to talk privately." He grabbed Smith's arm and pulled him to a far corner of the room.

"I think the time has come for me to talk to you," Remo said.

"Oh, yes? What about?"

"About Butterball and Blankey."

"Why does that bother you?" Smith said.

"Why does that bother me? All right, I'll tell you why that bothers me. For ten years I have heard nothing from you except secrecy, secrecy, secrecy. I have sent more people than I care to remember into the Great Void because they found out something they shouldn't have about CURE. Remember those? They were all assignments from you."

"Yes, I remember them. Every one of them," Smith said.

"So what are we doing here with this cretin?" he said, nodding toward Barry.

"Barry has been doing some work for me on the

CURE computers, to make them tamper-proof. And he understands entomology. I thought he would be helpful here in deciphering those notes."

"Wonderful. And now he has seen Chiun and me."

"Yes, that's true, since we're all in the same room together," Smith said dryly.

"And you're not concerned?" Remo asked.

"No. Barry is, well, Barry is different. He can't relate things to reality. He could learn everything about our operation, and never once understand that it involves real people in the real world. He lives in a computer-generated fantasy world. But I appreciate your concern."

"Well, appreciate this. When you want him killed because he knows too much, you do it yourself," Remo said.

"That will never be necessary," Smith said.

"I think it will be. Consider yourself on notice," Remo said.

"Thank you for sharing this with me," Smith said in a tone so bland that Remo could not tell if he was joking or not. He decided Smith wasn't; Smith never joked.

"So let's not waste any more time," Smith said. "What have you found?"

"You mean the bodies? You're looking at one of them," Remo said, gesturing toward the red-streaked walls and then to a dried puddle at the end of the room in which a skull sat.

Smith gaped in amazement. "That's what's left?"

"That and some spots on the rug. But the rug's downstairs with the other bodies."

"The ones your asssassins are responsible for, Emperor," Chiun said proudly.

"What did they do to warrant death?" Smith asked.

"They attacked first," Remo said.

"I mean before that. What were the circumstances?"

"There weren't any circumstances. That Perriweather weirdo told us to come here, locked us up with the lunatics and took off. There were two of them, a man and a woman. They tried to have us for lunch and we wouldn't let them."

"And they said nothing?"

"Oh, they did," Remo said. "They said a lot."

"What did they say?"

"They said 'Grrrrr' and 'Naaaarrrgh' and I think they said 'Sssssss.' Little Father, did they say 'Sssssss'?"

"Yes," Chiun said. "They also said 'Urrrrr.' "

"I knew I forgot something," Remo told Smith. "They said "Urrrrrrrr' too."

"The woman also?" Smith asked.

"She was as nothing," Chiun said modestly.

"Nothing if you call a bulldozer nothing," Remo said. "They were both as strong as gorillas. What's he doing?" He gestured toward Barry, who was kneeling on the floor scraping at the walls with something that looked like a tongue depressor.

"Preparing slides," Barry said cheerfully. He deposited the wall scrapings into a white envelope and flung his blanket expertly around his neck. "Where are the others?"

"He know what he's doing?" Remo asked Smith skeptically.

Smith nodded. "We'll need blood samples of the dead to check to see if it's got anything to do with the Ravits experiments."

"Ravits? He worked on bugs," Remo said.

"There may be a connection," Smith said. "The other bodies?"

Remo pointed to a small round table placed strangely, upside down, in the center of the bare floor. "Under there," he said.

As Smith moved the table aside, a swarm of flies buzzed into the room. The CURE director swatted them away with an air of distaste and peered down into the darkness.

"How do we get down there?"

"Take my advice, Smitty. You don't want to see the cellar of this place. Send the boy explorer there. It's a job for him and Super-Blankey."

"What's down there?"

"Flies, mostly. A lot of rotten meat." ·

"Meat? What kind of meat?"

"Cows, dogs, that kind. And two humans, or semi-humans, if the flies haven't picked them clean already," Remo said.

Smith shuddered.

"I'll be glad to go, Harold," Barry said agreeably. "If you'll just hold onto one end of Blankey."

"Harold, is it?" Remo said to Smith. "Sure, kid," he called out. "I'll give you a hand."

He lowered Schweid into the cellar using the blanket as a rope.

There was silence for a few minutes, then a soft exclamation.

"Barry," Smith called, covering his face as he peered down into the opening. "Are you all right?"

"It's fantastic," Schweid said.

There was some shuffling around, followed by a giggle.

"Okay. I can come up now," Barry called.

"I was hoping you'd decide to stay," Remo mumbled as he pulled Barry up.

Schweid came through the hole covered with flies and grinning like a loon. Smith made a halfhearted attempt to swat the flies away but Barry did not seem to notice their presence.

"It was amazing," he said breathlessly to Smith. "You really owe it to yourself to take a look."

"I don't think that will be necessary," Smith said, quickly moving the table back to cover the hole in the floor. "Did you take blood samples?"

"Yes, of course. But did you notice the flies?"

"Hard not to," Remo said.

"How many species did you count?" Schweid asked.

"We weren't counting," Remo said.

"More's the pity," Schweid said, grinning triumphantly. He pulled a white envelope from his back pocket. It was filled with squirming, dying flies, squashed together in a heap.

"Ugh," Chiun said.

"There must have been a hundred different species down there," Barry said. "There's at least fifteen in here and this is just a quick sample."

"Just goes to show you that a little rotten meat goes a long way," Remo said.

"Don't you see?" Barry said. "That's what's so unusual. Almost none of these species are indigenous to this area." He looked from Smith to Remo to Chiun. "Don't you all see? The flies were brought here. The meat in the basement was supplied to feed them."

"A fly hotel," Remo said. "Is that like a roach motel?"

"What are you getting at, Barry?" Smith asked.

"Somebody wanted those flies to be here, Harold."

"Perriweather," Remo said.

"He looked like a creature who would like flies," Chiun said. "Even if he did have a way with words. Egg-layer. Heh, heh, heh."

"What's he talking about?" Smith asked Remo.

"You had to be there," Remo said. "Never mind."

"What about the papers you found?" Smith asked.

Remo pulled a thick stack of papers out of his pocket and handed them to Smith, who looked at them and said, "They're some kind of notes."

"I knew that," Remo said.

Barry was peeking over Smith's shoulder. "Can I look at them, Harold?"

"Sure," Remo said. "Show them to Blankey too."

Barry spread the papers out on the floor and hunched over in the center of them, unconsciously twisting the corner of his blanket into a point and sticking it in his ear.

"Unbelievable," he said.

"What's unbelievable?" Smith asked.

"I'll need the blood analyses to be sure," Barry said. "But if these papers are right, all the deaths around here are the result of a fly."

"A lot of flies," Remo said. "We've got a whole cellar full of them."

"No," Barry said, shaking his head. "A special kind of fly. A fly that can change the source of evolution."

"Imagine that," Remo said.

'If these notes are correct, Morley made the biggest discovery since the discovery of DNA," Barry said.

"Is that anything like PDQ?" Remo asked.

"Don't be belligerent, Remo," Smith said. "Come on, Barry. We're going back to Folcroft. I'll get you lab equipment there."

"And us?" Remo asked.

"Go back to the IHAEO labs," Smith said. "Until we find out if Perriweather is behind all this and until we have him under control."

"No sweat," Remo said. "We'll have him under control."

"How's that?" Smith said.

"We'll just wrap him up in Blankey," Remo said.

18

Waldron Perriweather III sat in the middle of the sofa in his suite at the Hotel Plaza in New York City. The jeweled box containing the desiccated body of Mother Fly rested on the arm of the brocaded sofa.

Perriweather had moved aside the coffee table to make room for a small upright video camera mounted on a tripod. He leaned forward to adjust the focus, turned the sound level to medium, then sat back down. With his right hand, out of camera view, he tripped a level that began the camera running. He spoke earnestly, staring directly into the lens.

"Americans. Note that I do not say 'My fellow Americans' because I am not one of your fellows, nor are you mine. Nor do I count myself as of any other nationality. My name is Waldron Perriweather the Third and I do not count myself among any people from whom murder is a daily way of life, as it is with you. For, each day, you seek to decimate the oldest and most self-sufficient type of life which has ever existed.

"You are insect-haters all, from the housewife who carelessly, without thought, murders a struggling life on her kitchen windowsill, to the wealthy executives of the pesticide companies who deal out death in the billions and trillions each day.

"I am accusing you on behalf of the Species Liberation Alliance, in defense of the countless small lives you snuff out hourly without thought, and worse, without remorse. I accuse you."

He held out a bony finger, pointing it directly at the camera.

"Take, as an example, the small housefly. Maligned throughout history, the fly ensures the renewal of the planet in a way far greater than man can even attempt. Can you, do you, eat garbage? No. You only create garbage. With your food, your disposal containers, even your very bodies after your own horrendously long tenure on earth, you make garbage. The fly lives but a moment of a human's lifespan and yet he does so much more than any human.

"You regard yourselves as the ultimate creation of nature, but you are wrong, grossly wrong.

"The fly is the supreme conqueror of earth. He has existed longer, his numbers are greater and his adaptability is a thousand times greater than your own."

He lowered his head, then peered up intently toward the camera.

"And that is what I had arranged to talk to you about today. The adaptability of the fly. A particular fly, never before seen on earth, named by me *Musca perriweatheralis*. The fly that will restore nature to its original balance. The fly that will become lord of the earth."

He spoke for another fifteen minutes, then packed up the tape he had made. He placed it carefully in a box addressed to the Continental Broadcasting Company, the largest television network in America, went to the hotel lobby and dropped it into the mailbox.

Outside, the noise and clatter of New York City attacked his ears. People rushed by the hotel entrance, at least a hundred in two minutes.

There were so many human beings in the world. Far too many.

But that would end soon. *Musca perriweatheralis* would inherit the earth. And master it.

Back in his suite, he stroked the dead fly's back idly as he switched on the television set for the news.

"A bizarre report just came in from the wealthy North Shore in Massachusetts," an announcer said. "Police report that two bodies have been found brutally murdered in the home of millionaire Waldron Perriweather III."

Perriweather smiled idly.

"The two victims were identified as Gloria and Nathan Muswasser of Washington, D.C., and of SoHo district of New York. Police said the bodies were found in a cellar that was filthy and fly-infested and, as one officer said, 'like something out of the Dark Ages.' Police spokesmen said there is a possibility of a third murder as well. Mr. Perriweather, who is a well-known spokesman for animal-protection causes, could not be reached for comment."

Perriweather turned off the set with angry fire in his shallow blue eyes. The Muswassers' bodies. Three dead, not five.

"The Muswassers," he whispered in disbelief. Surely those two fools masquerading as scientists had not been able to kill Gloria and Nathan, not in their strengthened state. What had gone wrong?

Was it possible? Had those two killed them? Just who were this Dr. Remo and Dr. Chiun?

"Hello," came a sleepy voice at the other end of the phone line.

"Anselmo?"

"Yeah. Zat you, boss?"

"I'm at the Plaza Hotel in Room 1505. Come over here immediately and come right up. Don't ask for me because I'm registered under a different name."

"Right now?" Anselmo said.

"Right now."

"Ah, jeez, boss."

"Right now. And bring Myron with you."

When the two thugs arrived, Perriweather handed them a clear plastic container. In it were a few grains of sugar and a fly with red wings.

"I want you to take this to the IHAEO labs," Perriweather said. "Get in a room with two scientists named Remo and Chiun, then release the fly."

"That's it?" Anselmo said with some bewilderment. "You want we should deliver a fly?"

"That is correct."

"Like should we bash in their heads or something too?" Myron said. "I mean, we want you should get your money's worth."

"That won't be necessary. Just deliver the fly."

"Do we have to catch it and bring it back?" Anselmo asked.

"No. I've got many more," Perriweather said and began to giggle. The sound was so eerie and frightening that Myron nudged Anselmo in the ribs and pushed him toward the door.

Perriweather stared at the door as it closed behind the two men. It was time, he thought, to rid himself of Anselmo and Myron. If this Remo and Chiun had eliminated the Muswassers, the two brainless thugs should be no problem.

And Remo and Chiun would be no problem for *Musca perriweatheralis*. The container holding the fly was made of spun sugar and within six hours, the fly would eat its way out. If Remo and Chiun were near, they were dead.

He stroked the dead insect's back and then closed the jeweled casket.

"One of our children has already left the nest, Mother," he said. "Its work has begun."

An airline shuttle and a cab brought Anselmo and Myron to the parking lot of the IHAEO laboratories. As they stepped from the taxicab, they shielded their faces from the bright summer sun. "Wish I could be swimming today," Anselmo said.

"Tomorrow you can swim," Myron said.

"Tomorrow it'll probably rain. I should be swimming today, not delivering flies."

"We've had worse jobs," Myron said.

"But not stupider ones," Anselmo said. He held the tiny transparent cube up to the sunlight. "Kitchee koo," he said, scratching his finger tightly on the cube. "Hey, it looks like there's some kind of hole here."

"Where?" Myron said, squinting at the cube.

"Here on the side."

"That's all we need," Myron said. "Get a job to deliver a fly and lose the frigging fly. Put your finger over it or something till we drop it off inside."

"I guess so," Anselmo said. He took a handkerchief from his jacket pocket and placed it over the pin-sized hole.

"What's that for? You afraid of disease?"

"Maybe," Anselmo said.

"Stupid, that fly's been raised in a lab, probably. It don't have no germs."

"It still craps," Anselmo said.

Anselmo hoisted Myron up to the level of the window.

"They in there?"

"A young scrawny guy and an old gook, right?"

"That's what he said," Anselmo said.

"They're in there. But they don't look like no scientists to me," Myron said.

He saw the old Oriental, dressed in a tangerine-colored robe, sitting quietly in a corner of the room, scratching on a rolled-up piece of parchment with a quill pen. The young man was vaulting in a series of somersaults across the room, then hit the wall, did another loop, and landed on his feet soundlessly. Without hesitation, he did the same maneuver backward across the room.

Anselmo let Myron down to the ground.

"One guy's writing on wallpaper and the other guy's jumping around like a chimpanzee," Myron said. "They ain't no scientists."

"What do you know?" Anselmo said. "Let's get into the place, do what we gotta do, and leave."

"I'd still like to beat them up a little bit, to make sure Perriweather gets his money's worth," Myron said.

"No freebies," Anselmo said. "Paid for delivery, that's all we do is deliver. Nothing else. Like the Bible says, 'The workman is worth whatever you pay him.' "

The conversation was too deep for Myron, who walked away from Anselmo and began to jimmy the window of the room next to Remo and Chiun's lab. "We'll sneak in this way," he said.

"Chiun," Remo said.

"Leave me in peace. Can you not see I am busy?"

"What are you doing?"

"I am writing a beautiful tender epic poem about the ingratitude of a worthless pupil for his teacher."

"Well, this worthless pupil hears two goons outside the window."

"Yes," Chiun said. "And would you ask them to please restrain the noise? They make enough noise for ten."

"What do you think we should do about it?" Remo asked.

Chiun snorted. "I think," he said, narrowing his eyes, "that there are some details which even a worthless pupil can attend to without constantly annoying the Master of Sinanju."

"Sorry, just checking."

"Check in silence," Chiun said, going back to his poem.

Remo went out into the corridor to walk next door to the room the two men were entering.

As he did, Anselmo and Myron threw their bulk against the connecting door between the offices and with a crash of splintering wood staggered into the room.

Chiun rolled his eyes and set down his quill deliberately.

Anselmo roared at him, "Where's the other one?"

"God only knows," Chiun said with disgust. "Probably at the front doorway inviting passersby to come in and disturb me."

"This is the one that was writing on the wallpaper," Myron said. "See? There." He pointed to the parchment.

"Hi, guys," said Remo as he bounded back into the room through the hole they had just made in the wall.

"And this is the one that was jumping around like an acreebat," Myron said.

"What can we do for you?" Remo asked pleasantly.

"Nothing," Anselmo said. "We brung you a

present." He put the cube covered by the handkerchief down on the laboratory table.

"Good, a present. I love presents," Remo said.

"A fagola," Anselmo said to Myron.

"Can I peek?" Remo asked.

"Definitely a fagola," Myron said.

Remo lifted the handkerchief's corner and peeked inside.

"How sweet of you. It's a fly. Chiun, it's a fly. I never got a fly before."

"You got one now," Anselmo said.

"Anything else you need from us?" Remo asked.

"No. That was it."

"Good," Chiun said. "Then remove your big hulks from this room so I may continue my work."

"Hey, who pulled his chain?" Anselmo said.

"He's writing a poem," Remo explained. "He doesn't like to be disturbed."

"He doesn't, huh? Well, let's see how he likes this."

Anselmo stomped across the room, then planted a huge foot atop Chiun's parchment scroll and flattened it, leaving a tread mark.

"You've made him mad now," Remo said. He mumbled to Chiun in Korean.

"Hey. What'd you say to him?" Anselmo asked.

"I asked him not to kill you yet."

"Hahahahaha," Anselmo chuckled. "That's a rich one. Why not yet?"

"Because I want to ask you some questions first," Remo said.

"Oh, no," Myron interrupted. "No questions."

"You mean you were just told to deliver the fly and then leave?" Remo asked.

"That's right," Anselmo said.

"Don't go telling him stuff like that," Myron said. "It ain't none of his business."

"You weren't told to kill us?" Remo said. "Perri-weather didn't tell you to kill us?"

"No. Just deliver the fly," Anselmo said.

"Boy, are you stupid," Myron said. "He was just guessing that it was Perriweather and now you told him it was."

"You're pretty smart for a dumbbell," Remo told Myron. "You've got real promise. Where's Perri-weather now?"

"My lips are sealed," Myron said.

"How about you?" Remo said, turning to Anselmo.

Before Anselmo could answer, Chiun said, "Remo, I wish you would conduct this conversation somewhere else. However, for disturbing my scroll, the ugly one belongs to me."

"Ugly one? Ugly one?" Anselmo shouted. "Is he talking about me?" he demanded of Remo.

Remo looked at Myron, then glanced at himself in a mirror. " 'Ugly one' sure sounds like you," he said.

"I'll deal with you next," Anselmo said. He stomped over to Chiun, who seemed to rise from the floor like a puff of smoke from a dying fire.

"You gotta learn, old man, not to go insulting people."

"Your face insults people," Chiun said.

Anselmo growled, drew back a big fist, and cocked it menacingly.

"Hey, Anselmo. Leave the old guy alone," Myron said.

"Good move, Myron," Remo said.

"Screw him," said Anselmo. He started the fist forward toward Chiun's frail delicate face. It never reached the target.

First Anselmo felt himself being lifted silently upward. If he didn't know better, he would have sworn the old gook was lifting him, but he had no time to think about that, because as he descended he felt something ram into his kidneys, turning them into jelly. He wanted to howl, but something that felt like a cinder block severed his windpipe in one swat. Anselmo tried to gasp for air, as he realized that his bones were somehow being mashed. His eyes were still open and he saw his trousers being tied into a knot, and with numb shock he realized that his legs were still inside them. Inside his chest was a terrible pain. Anselmo thought he must be having a heart attack. It felt as if a powerful hand were clasping at the pumping organ inside his chest, squeezing the life from it. Then he saw that there was a frail yellow hand doing just that. He went into the void slowly, screaming noiselessly about a grave injustice that had been done to him, because he understood in the moment of his death that Waldron Perriweather had, all along, known he was going to die, and had planned it that way.

"Good-bye, Anselmo," Remo said. He turned back to Myron. "Where's Perriweather?" he asked.

Myron looked in shock at Anselmo's body, lumped on the floor, then looked back at Remo.

"He was in the Plaza in New York," Myron said.

"And all he wanted was this fly delivered?" Remo said.

"That's right."

"Remo, that one tried to be kind to me," Chiun said. "Return the favor."

"I will, Little Father. Good-bye, Myron," Remo said.

The big man didn't feel a thing.

"Kind of overdid it, didn't you?" Remo said, looking at the human pretzel that had been Anselmo Bossiloni.

"Do not speak to me," Chiun said, turning his back

on Remo. He picked up the flattened piece of parchment and brushed heel marks from it. "All I ask is for quiet and all I get is aggravation and conversation. Dull conversation."

"Sorry, Chiun. I had questions to ask."

Chiun again rose to his feet. "It is obvious that as long as you live I will get no peace."

He walked across the room toward the laboratory table.

"I wanted to know what the fly was about," Remo said. "It's from Perriweather, it must mean something." Chiun was peeking under the handkerchief at the cube.

"The fly," Remo said. "It's got to be the key."

"Find another key," Chiun said, plunking the cube into a wastebasket.

"What do you mean? What'd you do that for?"

"Because this fly is dead," Chiun said and walked from the room.

19

They were in the basement room in Folcroft
Sanitarium, where a small laboratory had been set up
by Smith for Barry Schweid. Through the walls, Remo
could hear the faint hum of the cooling system in the
rooms that housed Folcroft's giant computers.

Chiun made it a point to keep his back to Remo and
Remo just sighed and folded his arms and pretended to
look interested in what Barry Schweid was doing.

The little fat man was in his glory. He pranced
around the black lab table and whooped. He gestured
ecstatically toward the dissected speck beneath his
powerful microscope.

"It's fantastic, I tell you. Fantastic," Barry squealed
in his perennially adolescent soprano. "You say somebody just gave you this."

"Just like Santa Claus," Remo said.

"Amazing," Barry said. "That someone would give
a perfect stranger a gift of this magnitude."

Chiun snorted. "Not perfect," he said. "This pale
piece of pig's ear is many things, but perfect anything
is not one of them."

"Actually," Remo said, "I think they were trying to
kill us."

"This fly couldn't kill directly. It's been bred to function as a catalyst," Schweid said.

"Oh. Well, that explains everything," Remo said. "Of course."

"Why is this idiot talking about caterpillars?" Chiun mumbled under his breath in Korean. "Flies, caterpillars, I am tired of bugs."

"No," Schweid said to Remo. "The fly has no strength of its own. But . . . well, it was all in Dexter Morley's notes. Unlike ordinary houseflies, this one can bite. And its bite does something to the host body."

"The bitee?" Remo said.

"Right. It puts him into a plane with cosmic curves to which the body is not usually attuned," Schweid said.

"Say what?" Remo said.

"It's simple really. Take an ant."

"Now ants," Chiun grumbled in English.

"Can't we just talk about flies?" Remo asked Barry.

"The ant is a better example. An ant can carry hundreds of times its own weight. How do you think it can do that?"

"Chiun does it all the time," Remo said. "He has me carry everything."

"Silence, imbecile," Chiun barked. "Breathing," he said to Barry matter-of-factly. "It is the basic principle of Sinanju. The breath is at the core of being."

"Chiun, we're talking about ants," Remo said. "Not philosophy."

"But he's right," Schweid said.

"Of course," Chiun said.

"Their bodily systems are capable of refracting cosmic curves of energy in such a way that their strength is completely disproportionate to their body mass. Actually, any species could achieve this

strength, if it could muster the concentration for it,"
Schweid said. "It's just that ants don't have to concentrate. It happens naturally for them."

"You say any species could do this?" Remo said.
"Could you?"

"I think so, if I could concentrate." His apple cheeks
beamed. "But it'll need Blankey." He picked up the
ragged blue blanket and tossed it around his shoulders
like a warrior's cloak, then looked into space.

"I'm going to try to concentrate on the cosmic
curves in this room," Barry said, "and make myself
one with them." He took a deep breath, then another,
and another. His eyes glazed. He stood stock-still for
several minutes, gazing into nothingness, breathing
like a locomotive.

Remo yawned and drummed his fingers on his
forearm.

"Is this almost a wrap?" he asked.

"Silence," Chiun hissed.

"Oh, you can't be serious," Remo began, but Chiun
silenced him with a glance that would crack granite.

After a few moments more, Barry raised his head, a
look of exultation in his eyes. Tentatively he reached
out with one hand to grasp the leg of the laboratory
table.

"Come on," Remo said. "That's got to weigh three
hundred pounds."

Barry looked toward a wall, and the table lifted an
inch off the ground.

Remo gaped as Barry lifted the table another inch,
then another. The face of the fat little man in the baby
blanket showed no strain or effort, only innocent
rapture. He raised the table to eye level, his arm fully
outstretched, then slowly lowered it. Not one item on
the table had moved, not so much as a red wing from

the dissected fly. Barry set the table down without a sound.

"Excellent," Chiun said.

"I can't believe it," Remo said.

"I can," Chiun said. He turned to Barry. "I have been looking for a pupil. Would you be willing to wear a kimono?" Before Barry could answer, Chiun said, "You would make a fine pupil. We could begin today with the tigers' paws exercises."

"Will you cut it?" Remo groused. "Whatever this guy discovered, it's not Sinanju."

"Jealousy for the accomplishment of others does not become one who refuses to make the effort to accomplish himself," Chiun intoned.

"Who's jealous? I'm not jealous. It was a fluke. And I'm not wearing any kimono." He turned to Barry. "What has this got to do with the fly?"

"The fly imparts that strength without the concentration," Barry said, rubbing his cheek on the blanket.

"So those two people in the house . . ."

"Exactly," Schweid said. "You said they were like animals. They were. They were stung by one of these flies."

Remo turned to Chiun. "And Dr. Ravits' cat was probably bitten by a fly too. That's how he was able to tear Ravits apart."

Chiun was silent. He was staring at Barry Schweid, holding his hands up in front of his eyes, framing the young man as if measuring him.

"You have a little too much suet on you," Chiun told him. "But we'll take that off you. And the kimono is a wonderful garment for hiding hideous white fat, even though some hideous white people refuse to understand that."

"I'm not wearing any kimono," Remo said.

*   *   *

In the office directly above them, Harold Smith glanced at the bank of cigarette-pack-size television monitors mounted on his desk. They were kept on all the while Smith was in the office, turned to the three major networks and a twenty-four-hour news channel.

Smith glanced up from some papers on his desk and saw one man's face filling the screen on all four channels. He would have regarded it as odd had he not recognized the man as Waldron Perriweather III. Smith turned up the sound and heard Perriweather's droning hum of a voice.

"This is my demand of you, killers of the universe. All murder of insects is to stop immediately. I repeat, immediately. This will be augmented by providing insect breeding grounds in all possible locations, in order to make up for a consistent pattern of past prejudice against these noble creatures. Garbage and refuse are to be collected and assembled outside all human dwellings immediately. Garbage-can lids will no longer be permitted to be used. I hope this is all quite clear." Perriweather gazed coldly into the camera.

"If implementation of this demand is not begun within twenty-four hours, I will release *Musca perriweatheralis*. Its vengeance will be merciless. I have explained what this insect is capable of doing. I will not provide a demonstration for your edification, but those of you who do not believe need only ignore my warning and you will see the power of this noble insect soon enough. Unless there is complete capitulation to my demands, one nation at a time will be destroyed. Destroyed, utterly and completely, with no hope for renewal within your lifetimes. And once the action begins, it cannot be reversed. Nor can any of your puny measures prevent it. Nothing can prevent it."

Perriweather cleared his throat and it appeared that there were tears in his eyes.

He said, "We do not ask the destruction of your species, nor your removal from the earth. We ask only to coexist with you, as it was in olden times, when man was but a small link in a natural ecological chain. That was as it should be. That is how it will be again. Good night, ladies and gentlemen, you fiends of the world."

Perriweather's face was replaced by four newscasters. They all said basically the same thing: That scientists interviewed had said that Perriweather, while wealthy, was a crank with no scientific credibility.

Smith turned off the television and sat in silence for several moments. Finally he pressed a button that rang a telephone in Barry Schweid's makeshift lab.

"Come up here, all of you," Smith said.

"I don't think he's a crank at all," Barry Schweid told Smith after the CURE director had told them of the television ultimatum.

"Why do you say that?" Smith asked calmly.

"All right. Take it in order. We have Dexter Morley's papers. What they tell us is that when he went to work for Perriweather, Perriweather had already created a superfly. First, it could bite; second, the animals that it bit became super-strong and crazy violent.

"Ravits' cat was bitten and acted that way. The chimpanzees in Uwenda tore people apart. They were probably bitten. And it works on human beings. Mr. Chiun and Mr. Remo saw that at the Perriweather mansion when they were attacked by those two people. They had probably been bitten. So the fly exists and it was already a danger."

He looked around at the other three men, unaccustomed to keeping anyone's attention for so long.

"And now it's worse," he continued. "This red-winged fly is what Morley was working on, and he changed the fly so it can't be killed. Not by DDT or any kind of poison. It's impervious to all those poisons."

"You could still swat them," Remo said.

"It would take a lot of flyswatters," Barry said. "No, I don't think Perriweather is crazy or that he is bluffing. I think he intends to do just what he said."

"Hold on. If this fly is so indestructible, why'd it die before it hit Chiun and me?" Remo asked.

Barry shrugged. "I don't know. It may just have been a defective fly."

"Maybe they're all defective," Remo said.

"That's a big 'maybe' for mankind to hope to live by," Barry Schweid said.

Smith nodded. "Then it's clear. We have to stop Perriweather. If he releases these red-winged flies anywhere, he'll create maniacs, stronger than human."

"About nineteen times stronger than human," Schweid said. "According to my calculations. And don't forget. According to Morley, these flies can breed. They're not sterile. That means a new generation of them every twenty days or so."

"Like white people," Chiun muttered.

"So the question is, where would Perriweather strike?" Smith said.

"He might try a place where the insect population might be somewhat low but there are large clusters of people, targets for the insects. That's a possibility," Barry said. "Maybe," he added weakly.

"And maybe he has a score to settle," Remo said.

"Are you thinking what I'm thinking?" Smith said.

"Uwenda. He went batshit when we got rid of all

those beetles there. And if Barry here is right, it's got a low insect population," Remo said.

"I think you're right," Smith said. "It's going to be difficult to get into Uwenda though."

"Why's that?"

"Since the anti-American flap over the beetle business, Uwenda has closed its borders to all Westerners."

"If we can't get in, Perriweather can't get in," Remo said.

"Barry, will you check the computer?" Smith asked.

"Yes, Harold," Schweid said.

It only took the young man three minutes before he was back in the office. "It's Uwenda," he said.

"How can you be sure?"

"Waldron Perriweather bought an airline ticket to Libya three days ago. The ticket's been used. He went there. Libya flies into Uwenda. Our computer has a Libyan passport issued that identifies Waldron Perriweather as a Libyan national. Uwenda's where he's going."

"Us too," Remo said.

"If we can get you in without trouble," Smith said.

"Who could do that?" Remo asked.

"Ndo. The head of the IHAEO. He's a big shot there. He could do it. But he wouldn't. He's on an anti-American, antiscientific rampage."

"He could be persuaded," Chiun said.

"How?" Smith asked.

"This is negotiable information," Chiun said, casting a glance at Remo.

"All right, Chiun," said Remo with a sigh. "I'll wear the damned thing. I'll put on that stupid kimono. Once. Just once."

"I accept your good-faith promise," Chiun said as he walked from the office.

"Where is he going?" Smith asked.

"Don't ask," Remo said.

Director General Ndo was in his office, shining the wooden god Ga with grease from his own nose. There was a scream in an outer office, followed by a thump.

Chiun entered the office and with a sinking sensation Ndo looked past him to see his bodyguards lying in a heap in the reception area.

Ndo said only one word. "Again?"

Chiun nodded.

Like a beaten man, the director general packed Ga into his vest pocket, picked up a briefcase, and followed the Korean outside, in the direction of the airport.

20

It was a typical summer day in Uwenda, sweltering and fetid at daybreak and growing even hotter as the day wore on.

A bandstand had been erected in the square of Ndo's home village. The square itself was little more than a brown patch of trampled earth where the town's one public facility—a well once dug by a group of American volunteer students and now a monument— stood. Shortly after the American students left, the well had been poisoned by Ndo's brother, the military commander in chief, who mistook it for a community urinal, a mistake repeated innumerable times by the soldiers of his army. Another villager decided that the well's pump, once decorated with colorful grasses and rings of red pain, would make an excellent African artifact and sold it to a prominent European collector of primitive art.

Now the well sat unused and stinking, but the site was still where visiting dignitaries chose to speak as they incited the villagers to rise and to protect against Western imperialism.

When their motorcade arrived in the village, Ndo left the car and began talking to members of his native tribe.

Minutes later, he returned to the car and said to Smith, "You seek a white man?"

Smith nodded curtly.

"He is here," Ndo said. "A man arrived last night and has been seen driving throughout the area."

Remo looked through the car window with disgust. "Great. How are we going to find anybody in this barren waste? He could be anywhere. It was a stupid idea to come here in the first place."

"Then we can all return to New York?" Ndo said, ready to give a signal to his chauffeur to turn the car around.

"Not so quickly," Smith said. "The man we seek wants people. I think we should put a lot of people together in one place for him."

"Do you want to give away money?" Ndo said. "That always draws a crowd."

"Too obvious a trap," Smith said.

"Well, then how do we attract people?"

"Think of something," Remo said. "You're the politician."

"I know," Ndo said, looking at Chiun for approval. The old Korean's face was turned from him, however, staring out at the long bleak landscape. "I will give a speech."

"Keep it short," Remo grumbled.

The bandstand was hastily constructed from stone and wood once used to store grain, another imperialist ploy to entice the citizens of Uwenda into an alliance with the warmongering West. It was decorated with the latest flag of Uwenda, a pink-and-black-striped field on which three seersucker lions leapt. Ndo's aunt, official flagmaker to the President for Eternity, had barely had time to cut the lions out of the old dress used for flagmaking and to paste them on the flag with Super Glue before the speeches were to begin.

Villagers were rounded up at bayonet point and herded into the square.

When Amabasa François Ndo approached the speaker's stand, there was not a sound, not a ripple of applause, until the soldiers who ringed the square clicked off the safeties on their rifles. Suddenly the crowd went wild greeting the ambassador.

Ndo waved his hands in the air and grinned. His teeth sparkled in the brilliant sun.

"My people," he began.

There was no applause. He stopped, put his hands on his hips and glared at the General for Life, his brother, who snapped a command to the troops. The troops dropped to their knees in firing position, their weapons pointed at the crowd. A deafening roar of approval for Ndo went up from the throats of the crowd.

Ndo smiled and waved down the applause cheerfully.

"My friends. Four score and seven years ago . . ."

In the back of the crowd, Remo glanced at Smith.

" 'The Gettysburg Address'?" Remo said.

"You warned him no anti-American stuff," Smith said. "Maybe this is the only other thing he knows."

" . . . dedicated to the proposition that all men . . ."

Remo's eyes continued to patrol the area around the village square. Then he saw it—a jeep that had just stopped behind one of the small tarpaper-and-wood shacks that constituted the village's residential area.

He began to move away from Smith, but the CURE director restrained him by grabbing his arm.

"Look," Smith said, turning Remo's glance to the speaker's platform.

" . . . in a great civil war testing whether that nation or—" Ndo stopped speaking and swatted at a fly buzzing around his face. The sudden silence convinced the villagers that the speech was over. Unprompted by the soldiers' guns, they gave out one perfunctory cheer and began to turn back to their homes.

"Damned fly," Ndo shouted, slapping his fat little fists together.

No one saw the red-winged fly bite Ndo on the back of his glistening neck, but everyone stopped when he suddenly roared in anguish.

They turned to see Ndo, his hands balled into fists, crumpling the pages of his speech. He tossed the pages into the air, then spun in a circle, before beginning to flail about him on the bandstand.

He grabbed the pole holding the Uwendan flag and snapped it in two. Then he shoved the flag itself into his mouth and tore it to shreds with his teeth.

He jumped to the ground, grabbed a support base of the bandstand and shook it until the middle section of timber came loose in his hand. He crushed the wood to powder and the bandstand creaked and then collapsed around him.

The crowd watched for a moment, hushed, and then Ndo rose from the wreckage like some giant primordial beast climbing out of the slime, his throat emitting a sound that no human should have been capable of making.

The villagers, used to Ndo's long boring speeches about Marxism, jumped up and down in glee and began to applaud.

"*Musca perriweatheralis,*" Barry Schweid said excitedly. "Perriweather's here. He's released the fly. Do you hear, Harold? He's here."

"Didn't even give us the full forty-eight hours," Smith said. The CURE director looked to both sides. Remo and Chiun had moved away from him and were walking slowly toward Ndo.

The IHAEO official's brother approached the bandstand. He extended a helping hand to Ndo.

Ndo seemed to smile, then as the man moved within the reach of his arm, he swung his arm around in one long sweep and cracked his fist against the side of his brother's face.

Like a brown ball, the general's head bounded off his shoulders, bouncing through the dust toward the community well.

A villager screamed. Then another. The soldiers started to raise their weapons toward Ndo, but it was too late. The politician grabbed one of the riflemen, impaled him on his own weapon, and then spun the soldier around over his head.

He roared a growl as blood sprayed from the man, sending up little puffs of dust where it hit the sun-baked ground.

"Naaaaargh," Ndo roared, his eyes bulging wildly from his head.

"He says 'Naaaaargh' too, Little Father," Remo said. "Maybe that's how we'll be able to tell whoever gets bit. He'll say 'Naaaaargh.' "

"Good thought," Chiun said.

The villagers bolted and ran. They brushed past Remo and Chiun, as Ndo held the dead soldier over his head, and then tossed him, as if he were a light stick, into the midst of the other soldiers.

The Uwendan Army dropped its rifles and ran, and suddenly almost as if by magic, the square was empty of people, except for Remo, Chiun and Smith at one end, and at the other . . . Smith's heart sank.

Barry Schweid was standing near Ndo, slowly waving his blanket. The pudgy young man's eyes were glazed. Ndo looked toward him and his lips curled back in a savage parody of a smile. The fluttering blue blanket in Barry's hands caught his attention. Like a bull in an arena, Ndo charged it.

Remo and Chiun started forward but Barry shouted to them.

"No closer," he said. "I can handle this."

His body seemed to grow rigid and then his eyes apparently lost their focus and gazed off into a distance no one could see.

"Remo, Chiun. Help him," Smith snapped.

Remo ignored him. "He's doing that thing again," he said to Chiun. "The cosmic-power thing."

Chiun merely watched the battle unfolding before him.

As Ndo reached Barry and stretched his arms out to encircle him, Barry darted low, under the arms, stuck out his foot and sent the IHAEO officer sprawling on the ground. He thumped Ndo on the side of the head with one chubby fist.

"Dammit if that kid's not all right," Remo said. "Instant Sinanju."

"There is no instant Sinanju," Chiun said and moved forward toward Barry.

Ndo was on his feet again, circling around Barry. The little fat man had dropped the blue blanket as he turned, keeping his face toward Ndo.

Then, almost visibly, the strength seemed to drain from him. He was staring at the ground where Ndo's stomping feet had stepped on the blanket.

The young man paused. Chiun called out, "Here. Ndo. Here." But before Ndo could move, Barry dove forward to the ground to try to pick up . . . what?

"He's going for that damned blanket," Remo snarled.

Chiun ran forward to stop him but he was too late. One blow was enough. Ndo caught Barry between the

shoulder blades with a powerful down-crashing fist
and broke the young scientist's back with a sound like
the snap of a dry twig. Barry dropped into the dust as
if all the bones in his body had suddenly vanished.

He seemed to try to crawl forward a few inches. His
hand dug into the dust. And then his face thunked
down onto the ground.

Chiun was on Ndo, his arms and legs invisible inside
the kimono he wore, the flowing and swirling of the
garment making his movements look gentle and almost
slow. But there were the sounds. The thud and thud of
blows to Ndo, the crack and crack as bones snapped,
and then the African lay in a heap, his sightless eyes
staring upward at the sun, his hands twitching in the
final reflex of death.

Remo bent over to Barry as Smith ran up to them.

"Why did you stop, kid?" Remo asked. "You had
him and then you stopped."

Chiun knelt on the other side of Barry Schweid, who
offered a pained little grin.

He opened the palm of his hand. Inside was trapped
a red-winged fly. The insect was not moving.

"I saw this on the ground near Ndo. I jumped to
catch it so it wouldn't get away and bite anybody else.
Wasted my time," Barry said. "It was already dead."

"We're going to get you to a hospital," Smith said.
He knelt in the dust alongside Barry's head.

Barry shook his head weakly. "I don't think so," he
said. "Death is something tangible, something you can
feel. Did you know that?" he asked, his scholar's mind
still fascinated by the workings of his own organism,
even in its last moments of life. "Will you write that
down somewhere?"

Smith nodded, not trusting himself to speak, and
Remo said, "Where does it hurt, kid? I can take the

pain away." He realized that it was death he could not conquer.

"It doesn't hurt anymore. Not at all." He glanced toward Chiun and smiled again. "You understood what I was doing. It was the same thing I did in the lab, harnessing the cosmic energy. The same thing you do with the breathing. I had it, but then when I went for the fly, I lost it. Why'd that happen?"

"I do not know, my son," Chiun said.

"You said it was breathing. I was breathing right," Barry said. He closed his eyes for a moment in a wince of pain, then opened them again, searching Chiun's face for an answer.

"You breathed correctly," Chiun said softly. "But breathing is only one part of it. You did not have the training to sustain it. The power comes from the breathing. That is correct. But keeping that power comes from training, from knowing you have that power and that you can use it." He held both hands over his chest. "It comes from in here. But not from the lungs, from inside the heart. And from here." He raised his hands to touch his forehead. "Tell me. Was there not a moment when you worried that the power would leave you?"

Barry tried to nod and grimaced with the pain. "When I saw the fly. I wondered if I would be fast enough or strong enough to get it."

"That was the moment of your weakness," Chiun said. "In that moment, when first you doubted it, the power left you."

"I was so close," Barry said.

"You would have been a fine pupil," Chiun said. "You had wisdom and courage. You lacked only the confidence of knowing you could do it. That is the true secret of Sinanju: that a man can overcome any obstacle if he knows in his heart that he must and in his mind that he can," Chiun said.

"You think I could have been a good student?" Barry asked.

"Yes," Chiun said. "You would have been my best."

"Thank you," said Schweid. His eyes rolled up in his head and he saw Smith kneeling behind him.

"Thank you, Harold, for everything."

"And thank you, Barry."

"You're the closest thing I ever had to a friend, Harold."

"I feel that way too, Barry," Smith said.

Barry Schweid smiled once and died. Forgotten in the courageous moments of his final battle and death was the little piece of blue blanket which lay in the Uwendan dust.

Schweid's body was in the rear seat of the limousine that had belonged to Amabasa François Ndo.

"The jeep's gone," Remo said. "No telling where Perriweather is now. Do you think he's got more flies?"

Smith nodded. "He must have. Many more. I'm sure they've bred by now. He's got enough to carry out his threat."

"Then we've lost," Remo said.

"It looks that way," Smith said.

"I'm sorry," Remo said. "He could be anywhere by now."

"I know."

"Chiun and I will stay around to look for him, but I wouldn't hold out too much hope if I were you."

"I won't," Smith said.

"What are you going to do?"

"I'm going to take Barry's body to the American

embassy near the airport. They can arrange to ship it home. We'll bury him back in the States."

"That's a good idea," Remo said.

Smith nodded and stepped into the car.

"Good-bye, Master of Sinanju," he said. "Good-bye, Remo."

"Good-bye," Remo said.

Chiun was silent as Smith drove away.

21

"Well, if the world's all going back to the Stone Age, this is a good place to be, I guess," said Remo.

"How quick you white things are to surrender," Chiun said.

"Perriweather could be miles away by now," Remo said.

"He could be," Chiun said. "And he might be close by. Should one give up without considering the possibility?"

"All right. We'll keep following the jeep tracks," Remo said without conviction. They were moving along a narrow path through the brush, just wide enough to accommodate Perriweather's vehicle.

"And what of the curious condition of the red-winged fly?" Chiun said over his shoulder, without turning, as he continued to race along the path.

"What curious condition? The fly's dead," Remo said.

"That is its curious condition," Chiun said.

"If you say so, Little Father," said Remo, who had no idea what Chiun was talking about.

"Silence," Chiun commanded. "Do you hear it?"

Remo listened but heard nothing. He looked back toward Chiun, but the old Korean was no longer

there. Remo looked up and saw Chiun skittering up
the side of a tall tree, as quickly as a squirrel. The
Master of Sinanju paused for a moment at the top,
then slid down smoothly. As he reached the ground,
Remo heard the sound. It was an automobile en-
gine.

Chiun ran off through the brush with Remo following.

"You saw him?" Remo said.

"He is over there." Chiun waved vaguely in the
direction they were running. "The dirt road must curl
around through the jungle and joins with another road
ahead. We can reach him."

"Little Father?" Remo said.

"What, talkative one?"

"Keep running."

The road curved around a small hillock and then
passed through a dry dusty clearing.

Remo and Chiun stood in the clearing as Perriweather's jeep spun around the corner from the hill.
The man screeched on his brakes and stopped the car
with a skid.

Even in the bright African sun, Perriweather looked
cool and dignified. His hair was unmussed. He wore a
tailored khaki bush suit, but even at the distance of
twenty feet, Remo could see that the man's fingernails
were dirty.

"Mr. Perriweather, I presume," Remo said.

"Drs. Remo and Chiun. How nice to see you here,"
Perriweather called out.

Remo took a step forward toward the jeep but
stopped as Perriweather raised something in his hand.
It was a small crystalline cube. Inside it, Remo could
see a black dot. And the dot was moving. And it had
red wings.

"Is this what you're looking for?" Perriweather asked.

"You got it, buddy," Remo said. "Is that your only one?"

"As you say, you've got it, buddy. The only one," Perriweather said.

"Then I want it," Remo said.

"Good. Here. You can have it. Take it."

He tossed the cube high into the air toward Remo. As Remo and Chiun looked skyward toward the descending crystal object, he gunned the jeep forward.

"Many more," he yelled. "Many more." And then his voice broke into a wild laugh.

"I've got it, Little Father," Remo said as the cube dropped toward him.

He reached up and caught the object gently in his hands. But it was not glass or plastic. He felt the spun-sugar cube shatter in his hands even as he caught it, and then he felt another sensation. A brief sting in the palm of his right hand.

He opened his hand and looked at it. The welt on his palm grew before his eyes.

"Chiun, I'm bitten," he gasped.

Chiun did not speak. He backed away from Remo, his eyes filled with sorrow.

Fifty feet away, on the other side of the clearing, Perriweather had stopped the jeep and was now standing on the seat, looking back toward them, laughing.

"Isn't life wonderful when you're having fun?" he called.

Remo tried to answer but no sound came from his lips. Then the first spasm hit him.

He had been in pain before. There had been times when he had felt himself dying. But he had never before known the agony of being utterly, unthinkably out of physical control.

As the first seizures engulfed him, he reached automatically for his stomach, where his insides seemed to be riding a roller coaster. His breath came short and shallow, rasping out of his lungs.

The muscle spasms moved to his legs. His thighs twitched and his feet shook. Then his arms, the muscles straining and bulging out of their sheaths as his back knotted in agony. He moved his helpless eyes toward Chiun. The old man made no move toward him, but stood like a statue, his eyes locked into Remo's.

"Chiun," he wanted to say. "Little Father, help me." He opened his mouth but no words came out. Instead, he emitted the sound of a wild beast, a low groan that hissed from his body like an alien thing escaping. The sound frightened Remo. It did not belong to him, just as this body no longer belonged to him. It was a stranger's body. A killer's body.

As he watched the old Korean, he began to drool. The small figure that stood so porcelain perfect before him became an unreal thing, a toy, a focus for the inexplicable rage that was bursting from within every fiber of his new, unfamiliar body.

For a moment, Chiun, Master of Sinanju, teacher and friend, ceased to exist for him. He had been replaced by the frail little creature standing before him.

Remo dropped to his hands and knees and began to crawl across the clearing. In the background, Waldron Perriweather's laugh still boomed through the heavy humid air.

Remo tried to speak. He forced his mouth into the proper shape, then expelled the air from his lungs.

"Go," he managed. He swatted at the air. The next sound that came from him was a roar.

"No," Chiun said simply, over the roar. "I will not run from you. You must turn from me and from the creature that inhabits you."

Remo moved closer, fighting himself every inch, but unable to stop. Froth bubbled from his mouth. The pupils of his eyes were tinged with red.

The eyes again met Chiun's, closer now, almost within reach.

"You are a Master of Sinanju," Chiun said. "Fight this thing with your mind. Your mind must know that you are master of your body. Fight it."

Remo rolled onto his side to stop his forward motion toward Chiun. He clutched himself in torment.

"Can't fight," he managed to gasp.

"Then kill me, Remo," Chiun said. He spread his arms and lifted his neck. "I wait."

Remo rolled back onto his knees, then lunged at Chiun. The old man made no move to step out of his way.

You are a Master of Sinanju.

The words echoed somewhere deep inside him. And in the deepest spot of himself, he knew that he was a man, not some laboratory experiment with no will. He was a man, and more than a man, for Chiun, the Master of Sinanju, had taught him to be more, to see the wind and taste the air and move with the vibrations of the universe. Chiun had trained Remo to be a Master, and a Master did not run, not even from himself.

With a colossal effort of will, Remo swerved from his path. He had come so close to the old man that the silk of Chiun's kimono brushed his bare arm. Tears streamed down his cheeks as the part of him that was Remo struggled and clawed and fought with the beast that surrounded him. Shrieking, he threw himself on a boulder and wrapped his arms around it.

"I . . . will . . . not . . . kill . . . Chiun," he groaned, squeezing the rock with every particle of his strength. He felt the lifeless mass in his arms warm, then tremble. Then, with an outrush of air, expelling the poison from his lungs with a final, terrible effort, he clutched the boulder with his convulsive bleeding hands and pressed himself against it one last time.

The rock snapped, exploding in a spray. Pebbles and sand shot high into the air over him.

When the dust had settled, Remo stood.

Like a man.

Chiun did not speak. His head nodded once in acknowledgment and it was enough.

Remo ran across the clearing. Perriweather's laugh stopped short and Remo heard the metal protest as the jeep was forced into gear and started to drive away.

Remo ran, feeling the perfect synchronization of his body as it responded to the subtle commands of his mind.

The jeep puttered ahead of him at a distance, moving easily over the dirt road.

And then it stopped.

Perriweather pressed down on the gas pedal. The wheels whirred and spun but the vehicle did not move.

As Perriweather turned and saw Remo's hand holding the back of the vehicle, his jaw dropped open. He tried to speak.

"Fly got your tongue?" Remo said and then the jeep's rear end was rising into the air, and then it spun over and plummeted off the side of the road, down a hill, turning in the air, bursting into flames.

It stopped, flaming, as it crashed into an outcropping of rock.

"That's the biz, sweetheart," Remo said coldly. He felt Chiun standing alongside him.

"He is dead?" Chiun said.

"He should already be in fly heaven," Remo said.

They watched the flames for a moment, and then Remo felt Chiun's body next to his tense and stiffen. Remo himself groaned as he saw what had captured Chiun's attention.

A small swirl of insects rose in the air from the burning jeep. In the harsh sunlight, their wings glinted a blood red.

"Oh, no," Remo said. "There's more. And they've escaped." He looked at Chiun. "What can we do?"

"We can stand here," Chiun said. "They will find us."

"And then what? Let ourselves get eaten up by flies?"

"How little you understand about things," Chiun said.

The red-winged flies were blown high into the air on the rising gusts of superheated air from the burning jeep. Then they seemed to see Remo and Chiun because they flew toward them.

"What should we do, Little Father?" Remo asked.

"Stand here to attract them. But do not let them bite you."

The flies, perhaps a dozen of them, flew in lazy circles around the two men. Occasionally one would dip as if to land but a sudden movement of Remo and Chiun's bodies frightened them back into the air.

"This is great until we get tired of waving at bugs," Remo said.

"Not much longer," Chiun said. "Look at the circles they are making."

Remo glanced upward. The hovering circles were

becoming more erratic. The sound of the flies had changed too; it was uneven and too loud.

Then one by one the flies buzzed frantically, dove, struggled for a moment in the air, then dove again. They fell on the ground, around the two men, each twitching for a moment, before stopping as if frozen.

"They're dead," Remo said in wonderment.

Chiun had plucked up a leaf and was folding it into an origami box. Inside he put the bodies of the dead flies.

"For Smith," he explained.

"Why'd they die?" Remo said.

"It was air," Chiun said. "They were bred to live in poison but they lost their ability to live for long in the air we breathe. It was why that fly died in the laboratory. And why that fly died after biting that poor fat white friend of Smith's." He put the leaf box into a fold of his robe.

"Then we weren't even needed," Remo said. "These monsters would have died by themselves."

"We were needed," Chiun said. He nodded toward the smoldering jeep holding Perriweather's body. "For the other monsters."

22

A week later, Smith arrived at their hotel room at the New Jersey shore.

"Chiun was right," Smith said without preamble. He took off his glasses and rubbed his eyes. "The flies could not live in ordinary air. They lived in Perriweather's lab because the air was so purified and they were mutated to live in poison. But ordinary killed them."

"Ordinary kills a lot of things," Chiun said. "Great teachers are killed by ordinary, or less than ordinary, pupils."

His statement sounded, to Smith, like some sort of private argument between the two men so he just cleared his throat, then pulled a note from his jacket pocket and handed it to Remo.

"This was left for you at the IHAEO labs," he said.

Remo glanced at the note. It began, "Darling Remo."

"She says she's gone to the Amazon to try to find new uses for Dr. Ravits' work with pheromones."

"Gee, Smitty, thanks for reading it first. You can imagine all the trouble it saves me if you read my personal mail." He dropped the note in the wastebasket.

"You're not allowed to get personal mail," Smith said. "Anyway, Dara Worthington has been advised that Drs. Remo and Chiun died in a jeep accident in Uwenda."

"I never died," Chiun said.

"Just a polite fiction," Smith explained.

"Oh. I see. A polite fiction, like some people's promises," Chiun said, as he glared at Remo.

"Smitty, you'd better go now," Remo said. "Chiun and I have something to do."

"Can I help?" Smith asked.

"I only wish you could," Remo said with a sigh.

Alone in his office, Smith leaned back in his chair. Barry Schweid's blue blanket lay over an arm of the chair alongside the desk. Smith rose, picked up the tattered piece of fabric, and headed for the wastebasket.

If Remo could do it with Dara Worthington's note, so could Smith. There was no room in the organization for sentiment. Smith had dispatched his secretary's son with no more thought than he would have given the passing of a bumblebee. Or a red-winged fly. Barry Schweid was dead and he had been a useless, needy fool. His only contribution had been to make CURE's computers, in the rooms below and the backups on St. Martin, tamper-proof. Apart from that, he had been a troublesome childish pest.

Smith tossed the blanket toward the wastebasket, but somehow clung to the end of it. He felt its torn silky strands hanging on his fingers, almost as if Barry Schweid himself were hanging on to him.

He touched the blanket with his other hand. Barry had found the only comfort of his life in it. His heart felt weighted.

He squeezed the end of the blanket once more, for

himself, and once again for Barry, then let it drop. He put on his hat, picked up the attaché case containing the portable computer, and walked out.

"Good afternoon, Mrs. Mikulka," he said routinely.

"Good afternoon, Dr. Smith."

He was halfway out the door when he turned around. Mrs. Mikulka was typing with the ferocious speed that made her such a fine secretary. Her bifocals were perched on the end of her nose. Funny, he thought. He had never noticed before that she wore eyeglasses. There were so many things he never noticed.

The woman looked up, startled to see Smith still standing there. She removed her eyeglasses, looking uncomfortable.

"Is there anything else, Doctor?"

He stepped foward a pace, still marveling at what his secretary of almost twenty years looked like.

"Do you have any children, Mrs. Mikulka?" he said.

"Besides Keenan?" she asked.

"Yes. Of course. Besides Keenan."

"Yes. I have a daughter who's married and living in Idaho and two more sons. One's an engineer and one's going to become a priest."

Her bosom seemed to puff out slightly while she spoke and her eyes shone with pride.

"I'm glad, Mrs. Mikulka," Smith said. "It sounds like a fine family."

She smiled. Smith tipped his hat and left.

"I am waiting," Chiun announced from outside the bathroom door.

"Hold your horses, will you? This thing's as tight as the skin on a turnip."

"It is an excellent kimono," Chiun said.

"Yeah, sure."

"And you are wearing it to the dining room for dinner," Chiun said.

"That was my promise," Remo said. "And I always keep my promises."

Chiun chuckled. "Remo, I have waited years for this moment. I want you to know that you have brought sunshine into the twilight of my life."

"And all it cost me was the blood circulation in my arms and legs. Great," Remo said.

The bathroom door swung open and Remo stalked out.

Chiun staggered back across the room in disbelief.

His tiny silk kimono, hand-painted with purple birds and magnolia blossoms, covered Remo only up to mid-thigh. Remo's arms stuck out of the sleeves from the elbow down. His shoulders stretched the thin fabric to the breaking point. The collar opening, neat and taut around Chiun's small neck, jutted open on Remo almost to his navel. Remo was barefoot. His knees shone white next to the smooth colors of the garment.

"You look like an idiot," Chiun said.

"I told you I would."

"You look like that impertinent creature who sings about the good ship *Lollipop*."

"Tell me about it," Remo growled.

"I will go no place with you looking like such an imbecile."

Remo hesitated. It was an opening. "Oh, no," he said. "A deal's a deal. I promised you I would wear this and I'm wearing it to dinner. That's it, case closed."

"Not with me, you're not," Chiun said.

"Oh yes, I am. And if anybody laughs, they're dead." He walked toward the door of their room. "Let's go," he said.

Chiun stepped alongside him. "All right," he said reluctantly. "If you insist."

But at the doorway Chiun stopped.

"Hold," he shouted. "What is that smell?"

"What smell?" Remo said. "I don't smell anything."

"That smell like a pleasure house. Wait. It comes from you."

Remo bent his head over and sniffed his chest.

"Oh, that. I always use that. That's my after-shower splash."

"I did not know they made such things from garlic," Chiun said.

"It's not garlic. It's fresh. Woodsy, kind of. I wear it all the time."

"You wear it all the time when you keep yourself wrapped in clothing. That muffles your odor. But now . . . with your skin exposed . . " He pinched his nostrils shut. "It is more than I can bear."

His eyes widened into two hazel marbles.

"Quick. It is befouling my beautiful kimono. Quick. Remove it before the fabric is forever impregnated with that stench."

"You sure you want me to do this, Chiun?" Remo asked.

"Please, Remo. Now. Hurry. Before I expire."

Remo walked back into the bathroom. A moment later, he was back wearing his usual black T-shirt, chinos and leather loafers.

"Did you hang my kimono up to air out?" Chiun asked.

"Yes. Can we go and eat now?"

"Yes, if our appetites have not been ruined for all time," Chiun said.

"I'll eat just fine," Remo said with a smile.

Thrilling Reading from SIGNET

(0451)

- [ ] **ON WINGS OF EAGLES by Ken Follett.** (131517—$4.50)*
- [ ] **THE MAN FROM ST. PETERSBURG by Ken Follett.** (124383—$3.95)*
- [ ] **EYE OF THE NEEDLE by Ken Follett.** (124308—$3.95)*
- [ ] **TRIPLE by Ken Follett.** (127900—$3.95)*
- [ ] **THE KEY TO REBECCA by Ken Follett.** (127889—$3.95)*
- [ ] **EXOCET by Jack Higgins.** (130448—$3.95)†
- [ ] **DARK SIDE OF THE STREET by Jack Higgins.** (128613—$2.95)†
- [ ] **TOUCH THE DEVIL by Jack Higgins.** (124685—$3.95)†
- [ ] **THE TEARS OF AUTUMN by Charles McCarry.** (131282—$3.95)*
- [ ] **THE LAST SUPPER by Charles McCarry.** (128575—$3.50)*
- [ ] **FAMILY TRADE by James Carroll.** (123255—$3.95)*

*Prices slightly higher in Canada
†Not available in Canada

**Buy them at your local
bookstore or use coupon
on next page for ordering.**

SIGNET Mysteries You'll Enjoy